The Polar Terror

LIANA BROOKS

HEROES AND VILLAINS
Even Villains Fall In Love
Even Villains Go To The Movies
Even Villains Have Interns
Even Villains Play The Hero (Omnibus, books 1-3)
The Polar Terror

TIME AND SHADOWS
The Day Before
Convergence Point
Decoherence

NEWTON'S LAWS
Bodies In Motion
Change of Momentum (2018)
For Every Action (2019)

OTHER WORKS
Find other works by the author at
http://www.lianabrooks.com

THE POLAR TERROR

LIANA BROOKS

AUSTRALIA

Print ISBN: 978-1-925825-98-5
eBook ISBN: 9781386457527

www.inkprintpress.com

National Library of Australia Cataloguing-in-Publication Data
Brooks, Liana 1982—
The Polar Terror
138 p.
ISBN: 978-1-925825-98-5
Inkprint Press, Canberra, Australia
1.   Fiction—Superheroes   2.   Fiction—Romance—Science
     Fiction 3. Fiction—Romance—Clean & Wholesome

First Edition: October 2018

Cover Design © Inkprint Press.

ACKNOWLEDGMENTS

Books are never written in isolation. It takes a supportive team of friends, family, critique partners, editors, and publishers to get a book from "Hey, I have this wild idea!" to "Look at the pretty book I made!" This is where I get to say Thank You to all the people who helped make this book a reality.

To the home team… To my husband and children who listen politely while I ramble at the dinner table, read new chapters for me, and give me tactical advice for my fight scenes (and occasionally pose as dead bodies so I can describe them right); I am truly grateful. You make a good life the best life, and I love you all.

To the think tank… To my crit partners, publishing partners, and twins, who give me honest feedback and keep me from setting the manuscript on fire during the hard parts: thank you.

To the readers… This is, if I've counted correctly, the 12th title I've published, and that's because of you. Knowing that you're as excited as I am to read this book and share this story is the magic that gets a book past the "Well, my friends like it." stage of writing to "Look at the pretty book!" stage. I write for me, share to entertain my friends, and publish for you. Thank you for reading. I hope you enjoy *The Polar Terror*.

Special thanks to Patreon backers Gwen I., Clare W., Tonya C., Morgan K., and Florence B for their generosity, commentary, and willingness to jump into the story.

WANTED: The Polar Terror for a day of fun and crime with 7yo Everett at the Merriton Pediatric Hospital.

Everett is a sweet boy who has had a bad run of luck. He wants to conquer the mountains with his favorite villains, and maybe rob a candy store.

If you're available, please email: andrea@canada.dreamcometrue.org

CHAPTER ONE

KADDY LEANED HER HEAD against the pale yellow wall of the hospital room, closed her eyes, and tried not to hear the constant whooshing and beeping of the machines.

The ticky-tick-tick of the heartrate monitor.

The two-minute beep as the IV dropped another controlled dose of pain medications that seemed to do no good.

The whock-whock-whock of the second hand on the clock.

There was no escape.

She couldn't even run outside to the snow and let that peace envelope her. Not while Everett was lying in bed, staring out the window at the flat roof of the parking garage, refusing to talk.

With a sigh, she tried to reach him. Again. "Do you want to watch some TV?"

Everett didn't move.

"We could play with your action figures." She pushed herself out of the uncomfortable chair and walked over to his bed.

Everett let her pull the plush Polar Terror doll out of his listless hand.

She bopped him on the nose with it. "The Polar Terror is coming! He'll walk right out of this storm and—"

Everett rolled to the side, crossing his tiny arms as best he could. His bottom lip quavered with anger and pain.

"I'm sorry." Kaddy put the doll back next to him. "We're going to find a way through this, Ev. I promise. And then we'll sew you the Polar Terror costume you wanted."

"There is no Polar Terror," Everett whispered, his first words all day. "Nobody comes to rescue you."

She rubbed his shoulder gently. "I know, bud. That's why you have me. You and me, we can handle anything."

"Not this," he whispered. "Not cancer."

Tears choked her. "We will," she whispered just as softly. "We'll find a way to make it all right."

Everett squeezed his eyes shut.

Kaddy slumped back. Even if—and it was a really big if—the hospital pulled off a miracle and Everett got better, she wasn't going back to a job.

Her firm had been very patient, let her take a leave of absence, but her boss was retiring and the incoming boss hadn't liked her. He'd questioned her education, her field time, her work ethic… And while the guy couldn't come out and say it, his tone all but screamed SINGLE MOMS NEED NOT APPLY.

She shook her head. Being a single mom hadn't been her choice. She wasn't even dating when Everett was born.

But then there'd been a car accident a semester before graduation. Her sister and brother-in-law were killed on impact.

The idea of being a working, single parent was terrifying, but letting Everett bounce between foster families wasn't an option either.

Squeezing the guard rail of his hospital bed, she stood up. One way or another, she'd make a good life for him. That's what moms did.

There was a tentative knock at the door, like the person on the other side was hoping they wouldn't get an answer, but knew they would.

Rolling her eyes, Kaddy cracked it open for the inevitable nurse.

Andrea, the ever-perky Dream Coordinator for Merriton Pediatric Hospital, looked at her with the world's fakest smile, wide, frightened blue eyes, and damp blonde hair that looked like she'd gone outside without her usual hat.

"Yessssss?" Kaddy dragged the word out.

Andrea squeezed through the tiny crack in the doorway and slammed the door shut. "Okay. Hi, Kaddy! Everett! It is so good to see you two!" The words were rushed, panicked, and had the forced joviality of true terror.

But this was the Yukon in mid-winter, not some American city where a bomber was going to hold them hostage. "Is… is everything okay?" Kaddy asked.

The only thing that would scare Andrea was a really bad diagnosis. Kaddy's stomach flipped as tears welled up in her eyes. She couldn't handle that.

"Just dandy!" Andrea's voice squeaked. "Actually." She faked a laugh. "Funny story. Everett has a visitor. And, I know he's been so tuckered out, the poor thing, so I was thinking we should reschedule. Don't you? That's great!" she rushed on, not letting Kaddy answer. "I'll cancel. He can come back some other time."

Not bad news then.

Everett rolled over in his bed, forehead wrinkled in confusion.

"Who came?" Kaddy asked. The hospital attracted an eclectic group of visitors. Usually hockey stars, medical students, and politicians on goodwill tours. But Andrea welcomed all of them with open arms. "It isn't the Maple Leafs again, is it?" No one this far north loved the Maple Leafs.

Andrea's head shook so hard Kaddy worried the woman was going to give herself a concussion.

"Okay…" Kaddy glanced over at Everett who was showing the first interest in anything since his chemo treatment two days earlier. "Is there a reason you don't want this person to see Everett?" She licked her lips and mouthed, *Is it child services?*

"Worse," Andrea whispered hoarsely. She leaned forward and murmured a name in Kaddy's ear.

Kaddy's eyebrows went up in surprise. "Like… for real? You—" She stopped herself just in time and leaned forward. "You found a cosplayer to play the Polar Terror?"

She couldn't keep the excitement out of her whisper. Everett was going to be over the moon.

"No." Andrea shook her head and glanced over her shoulder. The color drained from her face. "He's… he's not fake."

"Who isn't fake?" Everett demanded from the bed.

"Just say no." Andrea grabbed Kaddy's elbow. "Please?"

Kaddy shook the other woman off and looked at the door. There was a thin layer of frost on the door. A suspiciously thin layer. Like someone was intentionally cooling the door for a grand entrance.

She narrowed her eyes.

Would the Dream Coordinator come in here acting terrified just to sell the idea of a super villain at the hospital? Yes. Yes she would.

It's exactly the sort of thing a perky, cheerful-before-coffee, former cheerleader would do.

Kaddy crossed her arms and sighed dramatically. "I don't know, Andrea. Ev's had a really rough week. I don't think he should have visitors. Not even the Polar Terror."

The heartrate monitor screamed in excitement as Everett sat up like he was attached to a spring. "The Polar Terror?"

With a burst of cold air, the door fell inward. Ice crystals glittered as icicles formed on the ceiling.

That was some impressive special effects budget.

A man in the Polar Terror's costume stepped in, towering over even Kaddy, who hadn't been called short since she turned thirteen and shot up. The muskrat parka, a rabbit fur hat, a strip of seal skin, a fur pouch, beadwork on his boots… and of course the very modern black balaclava with the Under Armor logo.

The Polar Terror had come to Merriton.

CHAPTER TWO

OVER THE YEARS, KADDY had become quite an expert on the Polar Terror, the only super villain north of the 66th Parallel. Everett had all the comics, most of the collectibles, and quite a few Polar Terror action figures. She'd even seen the fan-made YouTube videos with teenagers mugging for the cameras in faux fur.

This wasn't a teenager.

Whoever was hiding under the Under Armor balaclava and behind the polished, wooden Inuit snow goggles was a tall man. It was hard to guess his build under the layers, but there was something in the way he walked that suggested he was in his prime.

There was a gravity to him that pulled her forward. The Polar Terror was supposed to freeze his enemies with fear, bring an Arctic chill to any place he went, not make her want to run toward him.

Kaddy gave her a head a little shake. It had been a long winter, and she clearly needed some social time with other adults.

She stole another glance and caught him looking at her. Hiding a smile, she turned away. This visit was for Everett.

Dr. Kobbler, the chief surgeon, wandered into the room, grinning like a kid in a candy shop as he stepped close enough to inspect the Polar Terror's costume. "Delightful. Positively delightful. Is this real fur? It looks authentic." He nodded sagely at Everett as he mugged for all he was worth.

The doctor was a good man, always taking time for the kids, listening to their teddy bear's symptoms, and treating all information with the appropriate gravity or levity.

"Another comic book hero!" The doctor clapped his hands.

"Super villain," Everett corrected in unison with Kaddy. "He scares people."

Andrea reached outside and grabbed a hockey stick. "Exactly why he shouldn't be here. Out!" she ordered, poking the man in furs with the stick. "Kaddy, Everett, I'm sorry for the interruption. We'll come another day. Mr. Old Crow isn't even registered as a volunteer yet."

The man frowned at Andrea.

"Oh. Wow." Everett's heart monitor screamed in alarm as he grew more excited. "Aunt Kaddy, it's him! It's really him!"

Down the hall, Kaddy could hear the nurse running in her nice, sensible sneakers. "Wait a second!" Kaddy held up her hands as Dr. Kobbler ambled over and shut off the alarm.

"Quite all right, nurse," Dr. Kobbler said as Nurse Duncan appeared in the doorway, sweating and panicked. "Not to worry, Everett just got a little excited. Could happen to anyone. Practically healthy. Like a run in the park. Everyone likes seeing their hero appear."

"Super villain," Kaddy corrected again. She and Everett were probably the only fans of the antihero who fought lumberjacks and oil speculators in the Yukon.

Andrea cleared her throat. "Right. Super villain. Which is why I don't think he should be here." She didn't even wink.

Kaddy paused. It wasn't that she hated Andrea. It was that she resented Andrea's unending perkiness, her can-do attitude, cheerful smile, and willingness to spend hours enthusiastically discussing anything any of the patients loved. It left Kaddy feeling like a monster.

She wasn't 162 centimeters with tiny bones and the metabolism of a hummingbird.

She didn't have delicate features of someone who had French hunters in their mixed heritage.

She didn't have a boundless well of energy allowing her to play along. Not right now. She wanted desperately to throw all three interlopers out the door, slam it shut, and sit down to cry.

But Andrea was putting on a good show for Everett and, right now, they both needed a reason to smile. It was all over-the-top, but it was sweet that they were trying.

"Please, Kaddy," Everett pleaded. "Please, can he stay?" His small, cold hand grabbed at her arm, squeezing as tight as he could.

She put her hands on her hips and studied Dr. Kobbler's cheerful smile and Andrea's panicked grimace. "I don't know, buddy. Super villains are super shady characters. I can't let just anyone in to see you."

"I'm safe," the man in furs said. She couldn't see his face but his voice was deep, luscious—anything but safe.

It wasn't intentional, but she found herself licking her lips. Catching it, she smacked her lips together. "Ev, is my chapstick over there?" *Nice cover, Kaddy. The Polar Geek over there is going to think you like him.*

Ev handed her the vanilla-scented chapstick she'd bought at the hospital store because she'd lost her mint one in the snow last week walking across the street for a lunch that hadn't been chosen for its nutritional benefit. "Thanks."

"Do your eye thing," Everett said, swinging her arm back and forth so it bumped the rail of his bed.

Everyone looked over at him.

"My eye thing?" Kaddy asked, confused. "You mean glare at him?" The man in furs didn't look like he'd back down just because she was glaring. "I don't know if that works on anyone over eighteen." And the Polar Terror didn't sound like a high school cosplayer.

"No, the thing where you look at their eyes and say they're good or bad." Everett nodded.

His faith was endearing.

A few times, when he'd fought the idea of going back to Merriton Hospital, she'd told him she could tell if people were good or bad by looking at their eyes. She'd promised not to let anyone bad come near him.

It was only half a joke. Part of her believed in the skill in a way she couldn't explain. It was nonsensical. Unscientific. But a glance a someone's eyes and, nine times out of eight, she knew how skeezy they were.

"Okay." She nodded. "Mister Polar Terror, I'm going to need you to remove your eye coverings."

Everett gasped. "Wait! He'll kill you!"

"He's not Cyclops," Kaddy argued. "I do know my super… peoples?" What was the group noun for super-powered people? She'd have to Google that later.

"I don't know. Maybe he should go," Andrea said. "I like the idea of him leaving."

The Polar Terror shifted from foot to foot. "No one knows the color of my eyes. It's a secret."

That was true, for the comic books at least. "I promise not to tell," Kaddy said solemnly.

"You have to trade him a valuable secret!" Everett shouted, sitting sideways in the bed.

His hands clung to the rail of the hospital bed, and he looked like he was ready to chase down the Polar Terror if Kaddy let him leave. "It's in The Polar Terror number ten, where he fights the ice sirens. He shows Freezinia the color of his eyes in a trade for the secret of how to walk past the sirens and rescue the scientist trapped in the ice caves!"

Kaddy narrowed her eyes. "Didn't he turn around and kill her?"

"I didn't kill her," the Polar Terror said. "She drowned when her sisters took away her water-ice magic."

"Because she helped you," Kaddy pointed out.

Next to her she saw Andrea roll her eyes heavenward and mutter something that sounded suspiciously like, "Lord, give me patience. Amen."

Dr. Kobbler was still grinning ear-to-ear. The overacting was getting brutal in here.

"He tried to save her!" Everett sounded like he was ready to cry. "Please, Aunt Kaddy? Please?"

She looked down at his pain-thinned face. His eyes were two pools of darkness in sunken sockets. She'd do anything for him, and he knew it, but… "What secret do I have to trade?"

Everett's eyes filled with tears.

"I'll take it on promise," the Polar Terror said a little too quickly. He was obviously new to the whole acting-at-the-kid's-hospital thing.

With a sigh, Kaddy turned to him and raised an eyebrow. "What am I promising? I'm genre-savvy enough to know not to make deals with fairies or villains."

He stepped forward, blocking out her view of the exit and filling the room more than was humanly possible. "If I let you see my eyes, you promise never to tell anyone about them. In turn, you'll owe me one secret that is non-life-threatening, non-classified, and—"

"—impersonal?" She filled in. The promise of distance sounded like a good safety feature at the moment.

The Polar Terror tilted his head. "A secret you can share without hurting anyone. Personal is allowed."

Biting her lip, Kaddy glanced from Everett to the door, where the doctor and the dream coordinator were hovering. Everyone was waiting for her.

Closing her eyes, she nodded. "Fine. One secret promised."

The Polar Terror held out a hand, gesturing towards the dark blue privacy curtain.

Step into my web, said the spider to the fly.

"You don't need to do this," Andrea said as Kaddy reached for the curtain. "He can come back. Later. Much later. Or Everett can ask for a new hero…"

Kaddy rolled her eyes. "It'll be fine. Thank you, Andrea."

"Excellent, excellent." Dr. Kobbler clapped his hands. "Andrea, dear, we should get going. Let the family have their visitor."

Andrea stood there, trembling with dramatic anger. With a fierce glare, she lifted her chin. "Fine. But, Mister Terror, you better behave, or it's the Maple Leafs for you!" She shook her hockey stick with mock menace.

Kaddy covered a snicker with her hand as they walked out. "Somewhere, a sketch comedy troupe is missing a star." She smiled up at the Terror. "Come here."

He sauntered toward her and pulled the curtain between them and Everett.

Bravado kept her chin up—and a pinch of curiosity. It had been too long since she'd flirted with anyone. Since he was here willingly, she could play too, right? For a stolen moment she could pretend that everything was going to be okay.

The Polar Terror kept moving closer. Small, easy steps until he was within hugging distance.

Kaddy gave her very best Mom Glare. "Okay. Goggles off."

"Only for you." Slowly he reached up and untied the wooden mask. In the winter tundra of the Arctic, the thin slits limited light and allowed the earliest hunters to see, even if the sun reflected on the blinding snow. The Polar Terror held the mask as he looked down at the floor, almost as if he was bracing himself. He pulled off the balaclava, exposing high cheekbones and the deep tan of someone born and raised in the land of the midnight sun. His hair was black as a winter night and just as unruly.

He looked up, meeting her eyes. "Am I safe?"

Kaddy's breath caught in her throat. She'd never seen eyes that color. A deep black-blue in the Arctic Sea.

His eyes were the color of the ocean under the northern lights. The color of magic and promise and home.

Home.

Just looking at him, she wanted to run into his arms and break down. Start sobbing. Tell him everything that was going wrong because she knew he could fix it all.

Kaddy took a step back as she tried to shake off the knowing.

It was just her imagination, after all. Nothing real about it. She was reacting to being in an enclosed space with a very pretty man after a very long time being single. That was it.

No mystical connection. No destiny. No friendship.

The Polar Terror raised a dark eyebrow. "Well? Am I safe?"

Oh, hell no you aren't! He was the least safe person she'd ever met. He could rearrange her world with a smile, and she'd let him.

Kaddy nodded quickly. "Perfectly safe." If he heard the lie, he didn't say anything. And it didn't matter, she told herself. What mattered was what Everett thought.

Pulling the curtain back, she smiled brightly. "I gave him a good, hard look, Everett."

"And?" Her nephew waited breathlessly for the verdict.

"Everett, meet the Polar Terror. The Yukon's only super villain."

CHAPTER THREE

CODY HESITATED. THE MONIKER 'Polar Terror' had little to do with his actions and everything to do with his eyes. People said his eyes filled them with dread.

Even as a child, people had avoided looking at his eyes. Teachers had turned away. Prospective foster parents had taken one look and asked who else was available. Classmates had avoided him. A single glance was enough to leave people frozen in fear.

Shaking.

Quivering.

Crying.

Kaddy had stopped breathing when she'd looked at him. Stepped away. Done everything to demonstrate that she didn't want him closer. He'd expected her to scream, but there she was, holding onto the rail of the hospital bed like it was a life raft, waiting for him to come closer.

Little Everett, sickly thin in the pale green hospital gown, smiled up like an angel returning to heaven.

Cody adjusted his mask again. "You know, I've never met a fan before." He took a cautious step forward, watching for Kaddy's reaction.

She smiled tightly and nodded, waving for him to approach.

"I have to be your fan," Everett said. "You're the only superhero like me!"

"We're mostly Tlingit," Kaddy said quickly. "With a bit of Tachone. Drew was mostly Gwich'in."

"You're Gwich'in!" Everett said happily.

Cody nodded. "Old Crow. That's me."

"I'll let you two talk," Kaddy said. She shot him another small smile before retreating across the room to the narrow, cushioned bench that probably doubled as her bed while Everett stayed in the hospital.

Cody frowned slightly, then pulled the single guest chair over to the side of the bed. "So... how does this work? I've never officially visited someone before."

"We talk," Everett said. "Read comics. Sometimes people bring a toy for the patient. Then we go on our adventure. That's the important part." The little boy's gaze jumped to Kaddy as she put in headphones and turned something on on her tablet. "She's watching training videos for work," he said with certainty.

"Do you want her not to?"

Everett shook his head violently. "No! She can't hear this part." His hand was feather-light when he rested it on Cody's arm. "We have to go rob a candy store." The expression on the boy's face was a solemn mix of conviction and desperation.

Cody frowned. "All right. There are a few problems with that plan. First off, we actually need a plan. Second, there isn't a candy store anywhere near here. Third, I may be a super villain but I usually don't steal things. I scare people. There's a moral difference there."

Everett rolled his eyes in exasperation. "You're the Polar Terror! You don't let bad rules stand in the way of doing what's right!"

"Robbing a candy store so you can get cavities isn't exactly Right." Cody shrugged off his fur parka, shut his eyes tight as he took off the baclava and googles, then put the wooden googles firmly back in place so he didn't terrify his tiny fan. "Okay. Start at the top. Why do you want to rob a candy store?"

"Because Kaddy hates cake." Everett sat there in the following silence as if the nonsensical sentence explained everything.

Cody waited for a minute. He tried running the sentence through a few variants to allow for a child's lack of linguistic skills. Still, it didn't work. "What does hating cake have to do with anything?"

"Aunt Kaddy never celebrates her birthday. Last year I asked her every month when her birthday was, but she always said she'd just had it, or not yet, or we'd just missed it. She would never tell me the day. And she never eats cake, not even on my birthday. She says it's bad luck for her to eat cake."

"Gluten intolerance?" Cody guessed.

Everett shook his head. "She eats everything but cake. One time I heard her say if she eats cake, people die."

"Your aunt can read people's minds by looking them in the eye *and* kill them by eating cake?" He looked over at Kaddy in her standard Yukon boots, jeans, and a flannel shirt pulled over a tank top. "Are you sure she's not a superhero?"

"She says the only super about her is that she's super ordinary."

Cody watched her for a breath too long, then slammed the brakes on that train of thought. He had definitely not come to the hospital to flirt with some sick kid's guardian. "I don't think ordinary is the word I'd use."

Everett giggled, that whole-body giggle that only little kids could do. "That's what the doctor said."

"Which doctor?"

"The young one she scared away. He was a resident, but he didn't live here." Everett shrugged away the mystery. "Aunt Kaddy looked him in the eye and said, 'Never in this lifetime.' and then he transferred to a new hospital because she's scary." He paused and looked at his aunt.

Cody nodded and tried to find the thread of conversation again. "I guess you can't be scary and a superhero. I'm scary, that's my big thing, that's why I'm a super villain."

"Batman is scary!" Everett argued.

"Yeah, but Batman isn't exactly a superhero either. He's more a vigilante with gadgets."

"Then why do people call him a superhero?"

"Because he's white?" Cody guessed.

"Really?" Everett's voice was loud enough to draw Kaddy's attention.

She frowned up at them. "Is everything okay?" she asked as she took an earbud out.

"The Polar Terror was talking about Batman," Everett said.

"The Terror would win that fight," Kaddy said matter-of-factly.

Cody smiled. "Really?"

"In a fight with Bruce Wayne? Anybody in this room could kick his butt. The guy's a wuss. Take away his money and gear and what do you have? Nothing. If I can face down an angry bear, I can take out a boy in a bat suit." She put her earbud back in.

Everett nodded.

"Glad that's settled then," Cody said, trying to tear his eyes away from the woman who was stealing his attention. He gave himself a little shake. "Where were we? Candy robbery? No cake?"

"Aunt Kaddy's birthday," Everett said. "She's never had a party on her birthday since the accident. But I saw the date on the paperwork one time." He took a deep breath as he held back tears. "Mom and Dad died on Aunt Kaddy's birthday."

That sounded like a recipe for a life of guilt.

"Do you think she actually wants a party?" Cody asked. "Some people hit an age where they don't want to celebrate anything."

"Aunt Kaddy was born that age then," Everett said. "She doesn't do holidays. She doesn't celebrate. She just works."

"So... why do you think she needs a party?" He held his hands up in quick surrender. "I'm on your side, of course. One hundred and ten percent. I just need to know why we're doing this so I can help you pull off this caper."

Everett's eyebrows pulled in as he frowned. "Aren't capers the little green things they have on bagels sometimes?"

Cody blinked in confusion. Time for a mom-translation. "Um Kaddy? Miss... Kaddy?"

She looked up and pulled an earbud out. "Do you need me?"

"Capers as green things on bagels?" Cody looked over at her in desperation.

"Yes, at the fancy bagel shop we went to they had smoked salmon, purple onion, and pickled capers on a bagel."

Everett nodded. "We don't need to pull a caper. I don't like them."

"Caper can also mean theft or heist," Kaddy said. "From *capriole*, which means to dance."

An awkward silence filled the room.

"Don't look at me like that!" Kaddy protested. "I didn't invent the English language!"

"True," Everett said. "If Kaddy were in charge everything would make sense. She doesn't like it when things aren't neat and tidy."

Kaddy made a face of mixed embarrassment and frustration. "There's nothing wrong with being organized."

"Boys aren't organized! We're s'possed to be messy!" Everett looked to him for back-up.

Cody shrugged. "My house is pretty organized."

Everett shook his head in disappointment.

"That's because boys are messy and men aren't," Kaddy said without looking up. "You'll figure out the value of clean laundry when you want to impress someone." She put her earbud back in and went back to her training video.

Everett smirked. "Are you impressing anyone?" He did the little kid rock that was the universal sign of a child trying to look like a cool adult.

"Not really," Cody said. "I could, I've just never found someone I wanted to impress." Although impressing Kaddy could be fun. He picked up one of the action figures on the bedside table. "How about we play for a bit, or I can read?"

"What about Kaddy's party?"

"Hmmm." Cody nodded. "I think we need a multi-phase plan for that, kiddo. Good super villains always have plans. First, we have to make sure Aunt Kaddy really wants a party. Then we need to figure out what sweet treat she wants for the party."

"How are we going to do that?"

Cody looked over at their new target. "Act natural," he said. "We'll find an opening."

They re-enacted the battle between the Polar Terror and the Forest Fire at Lake Laberge, then Cody read from the graphic novels until Everett drifted off to sleep.

Once he was snoring, Cody quietly picked up his gear.

Kaddy looked up in an instant and turned off her tablet. "Are you done?"

"He's fast asleep," Cody said as she stood up. He couldn't help but notice she came right to his shoulder. The perfect height for kissing...

Stop, Cody. Just stop.

He was not going to entertain any entertaining thoughts about how kissable Kaddy was right at the moment.

"Thank you for coming," she said in a soft voice. "I know you probably had better things to do with your afternoon than spend it all here."

"Not really."

Her smile was sad. The hospital probably felt like a prison after a few days, and it was easy to imagine how miserable they both were sitting here instead of being at home.

"When is a good time to come back?" Cody asked.

"Come... back?" Kaddy looked up in surprise. If he hadn't had his goggles on, she would have made eye contact. Voluntarily.

"Um... Do you not want me to come back? I kinda promised Everett I would."

She shook her head quickly. "No. I mean, you're welcome to. I just figured you'd be busy. Merriton isn't exactly near anything, and you're not a local."

"How do you know that?"

Kaddy gave him a Look perfected by the first female mammal when she saw a male mammal asking something senseless. It said, *Did you really just ask something that stupid?*

"I know all the locals," Kaddy said, tapping her head. "And I have a good memory for faces. Someone as—" She bit off the end of the sentence and pressed her lips together.

"As what?"

Her cheeks flushed pink and Cody grinned.

"As cute? As handsome?"

"Stunning," Kaddy said. "I was going to say stunning."

Cody chuckled and dipped his head in embarrassment. His cheeks burned.

"Oh, please. You know you're hot. And in a tiny town like this every single person would know you if you were local. So you gave up your whole day to drive out here, dressed like that."

"What's wrong with my clothes?" Cody protested.

"Who wears traditional clothes all the time?"

"Someone who spends a lot of time in the bush and who doesn't want to freeze."

They glared at each other for a moment before Kaddy relented with an eye roll.

"Fine, you still went out of your way to be here." She sighed as she looked at Everett. "It's okay if you don't come back. He'll understand."

Cody looked at the small boy sleeping with an IV in his arm. "I'd like to come back. Do you mind if I do?"

"Can your schedule handle it?" Kaddy looked skeptical.

"One of the nice things about being a freelancer is I can travel and still get paid."

"What do you do, exactly?"

"Besides being a super villain who fights environmental threats?"

She nodded and rolled her eyes again.

"I'm a wildlife photographer and a back-country guide during the summers."

"Really?" Kaddy unfolded like a flower seeing the sun for the first time. Her whole posture changed from indifference to interest.

"Yeah, which means I'm pretty open this time of year." He took a step closer. "When can I come back?"

She hesitated for a moment, then stepped away and looked out the window. "Thursdays are usually his best day. He has treatment Tuesday and Friday right now. If it isn't chemo, it's physical therapy and rehab. But Thursdays are usually good." She smiled and tilted her head.

It was Monday now.

"I'll be back on Thursday." With a present for Everett and a reason to see Kaddy smile again.

CHAPTER FOUR

KADDY SAT BY EVERETT'S bedside watching a shroud of gray clouds roll over the mountains and into the valley with a fresh blanket of snow. The whole town of Merriton was being erased like rabbit tracks.

Laying a gentle hand on Ev's cheek, she ensured he was still asleep before closing the curtains against the bleak sight.

It was Thursday. The passes through the mountains had closed Tuesday night. Most of the hospital staff had been told to stay at home Wednesday. No one was going anywhere.

All around her, the hospital echoed, tomb-like, the quiet beeps of heart monitors bouncing off the brick sepulcher. She felt buried alive.

Taking a deep breath, Kaddy stepped into the hall and wiped away a rogue tear.

Letting Andrea bring the Polar Terror cosplayer had been a mistake. Breaking routine had been a mistake.

As long as she stuck to the habits of check-ups and meals, everything was fine. She could keep her emotions in check, focus on taking life one day at a time. One hour at a time.

Having someone break the monotony—having something to look forward to—put stress on her

defenses. For a few hours, she'd had hope for something better.

And now her heart was broken all over again.

Pressing her lips together and sniffling, she pulled
out her phone. At least the wifi was still working. The
internet got spotty sometimes during winter storms, but
it seemed to be holding up better than she was today.

She opened her Twitter app and scrolled through the
news. One of the American scientists she followed had
started posting pictures of lions with bad manes. The
Okeanos rover was going for a dive in an abyssal plain,
looking at new species that seemed alien.

Someone posted #WhatIWantNow with a request
for jokes. Most of them were weak, but Ev would get a
laugh out of them.

Kaddy sat down outside his room and typed in,
"#WhatIWantNow is Chinese food. Anyone want to
deliver orange chicken in this snow storm?"

A few seconds later a friend from Prince George,
BC, tweeted back, "Are you getting hit right now?"

"Snowed in," Kaddy replied. "Send an extraction
team."

"How about the hunk from *Snowed In With The
CEO*?" her friend teased, referencing a cheesy romance
novel Kaddy had sent her as a joke the winter before.

"No CEOs," Kaddy typed. "I want someone who
can go hiking with me this summer. Don't want to ruin
the boy's manicure."

Another friend chimed in with a GIF of a famous
actor winking with the caption, "Am I your type?"

"Ha ha," Kaddy responded. "Pass. I like them tall,
dark, and—" She stopped as she pictured the Polar

Terror. How to describe him? "—mysterious," she finished.

She didn't usually get hot and bothered by anyone. But him? "And I didn't even get his name," she muttered. Like an idiot.

Her phone flashed a warning that the battery was low. It always was these days.

She had a sneaking suspicion that her phone charger needed to be replaced. But that would mean a trip to the next town over, and she couldn't risk the passes closing while Ev was here without her.

It was probably time to do something expensive and order a charger in. But the shipping alone would eat half of her free-money budget—and then Christmas was coming. Ev needed a new pair of sneakers and something to put under the tree in the Gracie Wing where the long-term patients held their holiday party.

The phone charger would have to wait until her next paycheck, or whatever she got when the company terminated her contract in March.

With a resigned sigh, she put her phone away and leaned back, resting her head on the painted brick walls. Someone had tried to cheer the place up by painting a moose and squirrel mural. Somehow, she always started looking for Boris and Natasha from the old cartoons.

Her eyes drifted closed as the silence wrapped around her.

The scent of someone's lunch drifted down the empty hallway and her stomach rumbled. It smelled like orange chicken, the good stuff from the Red Fish takeaway on the edge of town. They served an eclectic mix there, everything from poutine to veggie burgers, to Chinese dumplings and tacos. The original owner was a retired war vet who ran the place with his wife and who labeled everything there 'American', as if it was a catchall term for Foreign.

Her mouth watered as the smell grew stronger. Maybe it was time to visit the nurse's station…

Someone cleared their throat and Kaddy jumped to her feet before she opened her eyes.

The Polar Terror stood there, looking awkward with a plastic bag with the Red Fish logo and a cloth bag full of what looked like craft supplies.

"Um…" Kaddy blinked. "I—"

"Is Everett still asleep?"

She nodded mutely.

"Do you want some lunch?" The plastic bag swung temptingly in his grasp.

"I didn't think you'd make it." Her gaze was riveted on the food. "I…" She shook her head and remembered her manners. "You're probably starving. How far did you have to drive to get around the passes?"

The Polar Terror tilted his masked face. "Around the passes?"

"They're closed," she said, then mentally cursed herself. Of course they were closed. Everyone knew they were closed. There'd been weather and travel advisories updating every thirty minutes on every possible form of communication. She'd just made herself look like an idiot in front of the only eligible bachelor in two hundred kilometers.

Unless you counted Dave over at the truck stop, which she didn't.

Feeling every lost minute of sleep from the past month, she focused on the bag of food. "You should eat. I don't want to steal from you."

"I may not have had the best reputation in school, but I did pass kindergarten," the Polar Terror said. "I know how to share."

The spicy aroma of orange chicken tempted her. "Is there enough for two?"

"There's probably enough for ten."

Kaddy let it go. It wasn't like she could look more pathetic. "Then, sure, let's eat. There's a table in the room we can use."

"Will it wake Everett up?"

She shook her head. "Days like this he won't wake up for anything. You can run a stampede through here and he'd keep snoring."

The Polar Terror smiled as she opened the door to the small hospital room.

Everett's bed sat near the window, framed by monitors and machines. There was a small bench with a faded green cushion under the window for days when he felt like being out of bed. The chair that folded into her cot at night was pushed against the wall next to the door, and, aside from the small bathroom and the free-standing wardrobe, that was it.

"Home sweet hospital room," Kaddy said as she pulled the curtain between the improvised dining area and Everett. "All the problems of a cheap motel room and none of the amenities." She looked at the small, rolling table used for Everett's meals. "This probably isn't big enough for two."

"Picnic on the floor?" the Polar Terror suggested.

She nodded, then stopped. "This is getting ridiculous. What am I supposed to call you? The Polar Terror? Just Polar Terror? Polar? Mister Terror?"

He set the bag of craft supplies on her chair and the food on the floor. "How about Cody?"

"Is that your name?"

"It's short for Kodiak, but I spell Cody with a C. Blame the foster dad I had when I was five. He thought Kody with a K sounded pretentious."

Kaddy shrugged. "You're talking to someone who has a weird name because my great-great-great-grandma couldn't spell Katie right."

"I like Kaddy. It's unique."

"I've heard that pick-up line before." She gestured to his coat and gear. "Don't you want to take that off? It's not cold in here. You have to be boiling."

Cody chuckled. "First you tell me not to use pick-up lines and then you tell me to take my clothes off," he teased.

Her cheeks flushed with embarrassment. "I just meant—"

"I know. I know," he said as he took off his coat. His hand stopped by the wooden mask over his eyes. "Um, do you want to turn around?"

"Why? I've already seen the color of your eyes and Everett's asleep. You don't need to stay in character."

There was a pause in the conversation that stretched past the point of comfortable.

"Fine," Cody said finally. "As long as you don't mind."

"Not at all. Make yourself comfortable."

Cody tossed his fur coat on the chair, followed quickly by the wooden mask, balaclava, and a heavy sweater. He was as fit and muscular as she'd guessed. And his blue eyes still made her want to stare in wonder.

Trying not to gawk like a lovestruck teen, she turned her attention to making a space on the floor for picnicking.

"Hope you like orange chicken," Cody said as he opened the white box.

Kaddy risked a glance. "Did you read my Twitter?"

"I didn't even know you had one, so, no. Why?"

"I asked for Chinese delivery as a joke."

He shrugged and sat down, portioning out a small bowl of rice and meat for himself. "Must be the superpowers. Sometimes I get little premonitiony thingies." With a disarming grin he winked.

"Or maybe the orange chicken down at the Red Fish just smells amazing." She inhaled the spicy, citrusy scent. "I've missed this."

"Getting tired of hospital food?" Cody asked between bites.

"It's not like I could drive anywhere in this mess."

He looked out the window at the wall of white snow falling down. "True. But it'll clear up by the time Everett wakes up."

"Doubt it." The chicken was as delicious as she remembered. "Speaking of driving, how did you get into town? I mean…" She sighed in frustration. "You shouldn't have come. The roads are way too dangerous."

"I stayed off the roads. Took a moose."

Kaddy blinked at him.

"They handle deep snow better than a dogsled team," he said as if it was an explanation.

She closed her eyes. "Do not repeat that in front of Everett. He's going to try riding a moose and get stomped to death."

Cody chuckled. It was a low, masculine sound of pleasure and amusement. "I'll stop trying to make you smile. That was my best joke, and I couldn't even get an amused grimace."

Guilt hit her like a truck skidding on ice. "Sorry, my social skills have atrophied over the last few months. I'm…" A sigh swallowed her awkward apology. There really was no excuse for talking to another adult like a child. It just came out. "I'm sorry."

"Don't be. You're stressed. This can't be easy for you, and it's not like the Dream Coordinator downstairs is exactly asking you to fill out a wish list."

"Definitely not." The idea of Andrea haranguing her to find a fillable dream sent a shiver of fear down her back. "Don't suggest it. She'd try."

Ocean-dark eyes caught hers. "Don't you have a dream?"

"Mmmm… does a tropical vacation count?" Kaddy shook her head. "No. I don't want anything really. Maybe once Everett is better, but until then, no."

"What happened? I know Andrea said a bone graft, but don't they screen those?"

Kaddy nodded as she ate. "The car accident that killed his parents crushed his shin. He had surgeries to rebuild it, and physical therapy, but the leg wasn't growing correctly. This last surgery was supposed to be the last. But…" She took a deep breath.

"We knew the donor. Collin Haskins, an old war vet who retired here to get away from everyone when his wife died. He owned some land outside Merriton. Used to come volunteer at the hospital, play with the kids, tell them stories, that sort of thing. He slipped on some ice last September, hit his head, and his kids had a panic.

They made him move to Vancouver. But it was in his will, any useable organs were supposed to be donated to patients waiting here.

"He died in October. Had a heart attack while was sleeping, so he never felt a thing. He was in his nineties, so I suppose something was going to get him eventually. The bone graft arrived the next day. Everett had his surgery. But then things went wrong. He wasn't recovering as quickly as they expected. He was tired. His blood panels came back with problems. Then Dr. Kobbler came in and told me they suspected bone cancer."

She'd gone a week without sleeping, consumed by guilt and fear. Knowing that she had done everything right didn't help. Every time Everett got sick, she wondered if her sister could have prevented it, could have anticipated it, could have done this mom thing better.

"He's a tough kid," Cody said quietly. "Seems sweet. What does the doc say about recovery?"

"He had another surgery to remove the tainted bone, and now a round of chemo. We're waiting on another bone graft I guess. And then? Who knows." She stirred the rice in her bowl around moodily. "He might get better. He might not. We won't know for a few months still."

"I'm sorry."

"Not your fault."

Everett stirred in the hospital bed and rolled over. "Mmm, that smells good."

Quickly forcing a fake smile, Kaddy got up. "Hey, kiddo, how are you feeling?"

"Sleepy." He yawned. "Bored."

"Want to go play outside?" Cody asked.

She looked over her shoulder to see Cody securing the wooden mask over his face.

Everett leaned forward and his face lit up with delight. "You came back!"

"I told you I'd be here Thursday, rain or shine."

"Epic snowstorms were not part of that agreement," Kaddy said tartly, "but he's still here."

Everett frowned at the snow outside. "Can we go out in this?"

"No," Kaddy said. "Sorry."

"It'll stop snowing in a bit," Cody said. "You need lunch first, and then we need to make you a Polar Terror suit." He held up his bag of craft supplies. "Caribou hide, rabbit fur, some bead patterns so you can pick out what you want, and a few other odds and ends…" His sentence trailed away as he looked up at Kaddy. "What? Are you vegan?"

"No! But," she stared at the supplies, "where'd you get this?"

He looked down at the bag then back at her. "Same place our grandparents got theirs."

"That's so cool!" Everett looked thrilled. "Is it warm?"

"The warmest," Cody promised.

Kaddy rolled her eyes up and tried not to think about how much this all cost in time and labor.

She couldn't really stop Cody from forging ahead with his Polar Terror act. But that wouldn't stop her from dropping a few subtle hints that he could keep his spending to a minimum though.

"I'll go get Nurse Meg," Kaddy said. "If there's sunshine outside after lunch, we'll talk about going outside for a short walk. But not if the temperature is too low."

"It won't be too cold," Cody said as if it were a promise.

"It was thirty below an hour ago," Kaddy retorted. "Let's manage our expectations here."

The fake super villain sighed dramatically. "How cold is too cold for going outside?"

"Anything below minus twenty C."

He nodded.

Sunlight pierced the window, shattering the clouds. As Kaddy watched, the storm fled. The little hospital in Merriton was bathed in warm sunshine. On the window sill, the mercury in the thermometer started to climb.

Everett clapped with joy. "How did you do that?"

Cody shrugged. "Super powers."

Kaddy glared at him.

"And knowing a very accurate meteorologist," Cody said quickly. "I knew it would get sunny this afternoon and didn't want to leave you upset."

She rolled her eyes.

"I'm certain the roads are perfectly safe too," he added. "I always consider safety before I do anything."

It was such a perfectly melodramatic statement that Kaddy had to fight a snicker. At least he was putting on the act of Responsible Adult for Everett. But the way his mouth twitched up in a half-smile? That felt like it was for her.

Tonight, she'd tell her Twitter friends how she spent the day snowed in with a super villain.

CHAPTER FIVE

EVERETT LAUGHED AS HE flew down a hill of snow.

Framed by the bright blue winter sky, Kaddy sparkled like gold in a Yukon river.

For the past hour, Cody had been fighting with himself. It was a timing issue, really. If he'd met Kaddy somewhere else, through work or on a hike or at a bar, he wouldn't have hesitated. Her smile was too warm, the gaze in her eyes too inviting, and he wanted to say yes to the silent question. Take her to dinner, with Everett in tow, go snowshoeing and make them hot chocolate.

It was easy to picture a first kiss, won with whispers and smiles, and snuck in when Everett wasn't watching.

He could picture Kaddy's shy smile as she tucked her hair behind her ear.

He licked his lips and could almost taste the vanilla lip balm she'd applied earlier.

"You shouldn't do that," Everett said.

Startled, Cody looked down at him. "Do what now?"

"You shouldn't lick your lips. Aunt Kaddy says that's how they get chapped and cracked. You'll bleed."

"Oh." Cody nodded. "She's right. I shouldn't do that." Shouldn't have been thinking about her kiss, either.

Timing was the thing.

Flirting with Kaddy while her nephew was in a hospital bed felt insensitive.

But then she was walking toward them, smiling, and when a flurry of snow drifted past shaped like a wedding dress, he realized he had a serious problem.

"What are you two being so serious about?" Kaddy asked. "We only have a half-hour of daylight left!"

"I was—"

"He was licking his lips!" Everett reported.

Kaddy's gaze swept across his lips, and hers puckered ever so slightly in invitation.

He gritted his teeth as he resisted the urge to take her up on the invitation.

"Would you like to borrow my chapstick?"

Off your lips? "Sure."

She fished the little white tube from her pocket and held it out. With a slight blush, she looked away. "Come on, kiddo, one more trip down the hill and then we need to head inside. The Polar Terror needs to get on the road before the bridges over the gorge ice up."

"The roads are fine," Cody said. They were: dry, clean, and one hundred percent ice free. He'd made sure of that.

Kaddy looked at the road skeptically. "The plow did a good job, but the bridges ice over and that's not a place you want to go off the road."

Cody leaned over and whispered, "I told you, I rode a moose into town."

She stopped, bumping into his chest, and looking up. Her eyes were a beautiful summer brown, the color of hawk's feathers and an eagle's eye.

As if reading his mind, she blushed and looked away. "This is ridiculous."

Yes, it was. But he was going to play it safe for a little longer anyway. "What's ridiculous is this coat. What is this, a knock-off of a knock-off?" He pinched the faded green fabric with a rip on the side. It was puffy in attempt to add extra insulation, but terribly made and it couldn't possibly be warm enough for a day like today.

"I got it at the flea market a few years back. It's okay."

"No." Cody shook his head and poked at the fraying edge of the pocket. "I need to make you a jacket too."

"You don't need to." She put extra emphasis on the word 'need' and there was a laugh in her voice.

He smiled. "I want to."

Kaddy made a show of watching Everett climb the hill in his heavy winter gear. "I admit, I'm a little envious of Polar Terror Junior over there." She shifted her weight—and her foot slipped on a smooth patch of ice.

Cody caught her before she could fall. "You'd look good in the jacket. Some beadwork… Hawks? Eagles maybe?"

She was frowning at the ground. "Where did the ice come from?"

"No idea," Cody lied. What was the point of being a super villain if he didn't get to use his powers for his own gains every now and then? And it wasn't like she was objecting to his arm around her waist.

Kaddy turned slowly and rested a hand on his shoulder. There were about six too many layers between his skin and hers. "You know, if you're trying to flirt…"

He braced himself for the rejection.

"You might want to be a little more obvious."

"More obvious?" There was a squeak in his voice.

She pushed herself away. "When there's a sick kid in the family it's hard to tell why people are being nice. Sometimes they do it to be polite, or because they figure you won't be around long. Sometimes it's to get noticed, like, 'Oh! Look! I was kind to that sad person!' So—"

"I'm flirting," Cody said. "Because you're beautiful and fun to flirt with."

"And I have a kid."

He nodded. "I admit I've never been married, but I've noticed that some families have more than one kid."

Her eyebrows knotted together in frustration. "So?"

"So I assume that means married couples still flirt and love each other even after the first kid shows up."

"Married?" Kaddy laughed. "Wow. You just… You skipped straight past everything to married? Really?"

"I said I was flirting. I didn't say I was good at it."

She laughed and walked away, shaking her head.

"Should I keep trying?" he called after her as Everett zipped between them on his sled.

Kaddy turned around and wrinkled her nose. "I don't know. It's kind of unfair. So much of communication is body language and facial expression. You can see me, but most of your face is hidden. That's cheating."

Everett walked up, pulling his sled by a rope. "What's she saying?"

"Your aunt is trying to unmask me. Again."

"We can do something without clothes next time," Everett said with a small child's sigh.

Cody stared down at him.

"We don't know there will be a next time," Kaddy said quickly. "The Polar Terror is a busy man."

He looked up at Kaddy. "Without clothes?"

"Like swimming," Everett said. "I like the pool."

"We need to get permission to take you to the pool," Kaddy said. "But maybe this summer. Once cold season is over." She reached for Everett's hand. "We should get inside. The sun's going down."

Everett glared over at the sun. "It's not even late!"

"It's winter. We get five hours of sunshine, and we're lucky to get that today. The forecast said the storm was going to last a few days." She shot Cody a glare.

Cody looked at the heavy clouds roiling angrily over the distant mountain peaks. "They look happy where they are."

"Uh huh." Kaddy turned her glare to the clouds. "Totally normal. Clouds always twist like that. In the winter. In the Yukon. Nothing peculiar about that at all." She dragged the word out.

"Is something wrong?" Everett asked.

Kaddy patted his head. "No. I was just thinking that our friend, the Polar Terror, is not so subtle some-times."

"The clouds aren't my fault!" Cody lied with a quick smile. It was nice to see Kaddy playing along.

Everett covered his mouth with a mittened hand as he giggled. "He doesn't really control the clouds, Aunt Kaddy! He's only a pretend super villain."

"I know." Finally a smile appeared. "He just got very lucky with the weather today, didn't he?"

Cody did his best to look as innocent as possible when dressed like an eighteenth-century fur trapper's illegitimate son.

The snow swirled playfully around him. It probably wasn't helping.

If he'd actually been born in the eighteenth century, he would have been burned as a witch—unless that happened earlier. He'd never been good about attending school, and when he'd gone to history class, he'd been so bored he'd fallen asleep.

Still, he'd picked up enough to know that he should be grateful for modern movies, CGI, and the deeply cynical nature of everyone who'd ever read the internet. It meant that people assumed there was a trick instead of believing he could control the snow.

"Come on," Cody said. "I bet they have snacks waiting for you."

Everett rolled his eyes. "They have medications and protein-enriched pudding. I hate it." The little boy looked up with puppy dog eyes. "Can we go rob a candy store now?"

"Nice try," Kaddy said. "In we go." She tried to herd Everett forward, but he stuck by Cody's side.

Cody gave him a nudge. "I think your aunt's feeling unappreciated."

The kid looked up between them. "Aunt Kaddy, can I talk to him alone?"

Kaddy hesitated, then nodded. "Sure. I'll go up ahead and put the sled away." She took the rope. "I'll be right in the atrium, watching, if you need me."

Everett nodded solemnly.

Kaddy flashed them a smile and marched on ahead.

"I'm sorry," Cody said. Timing. It was always the timing. "I should have been paying attention to you, huh?"

"Oh, I'm fine," Everett said. "I just wanted to see if talking to Aunt Kaddy worked. Did you get any secrets out of her?" Big, brown eyes looked up at him full of hope.

"Um…" Cody stared ahead at Kaddy retreating in the distance. Secrets? "Not really? I think she's kind of guarded."

"What's that mean?"

"I mean I'm a stranger. She may not want to talk about private things yet."

"Birthday stuff isn't private!" Everett protested.

Cody shrugged. "It can be, to an adult. We're funny that way."

Under the shadow of the fur-lined hood, Everett frowned. "Well, what do you do for your birthday?"

Cody winced; he'd been hoping no one would bring that up. "I usually ignore it."

"Is it 'cause you're old?"

"Not, it's just… not a happy memory."

Everett nodded. "I knew I was right wishing for you. Aunt Kaddy doesn't have a happy birthday memory. You don't have a happy birthday memory. Gosh…" He stopped in the middle of a snow drift up to his knees. "Are all my birthday memories going to turn bad too? Is that what happens when you get old?"

"No! No. Of course not." Cody looked across the field where Kaddy was lingering by the rack of sleds. "Listen, it's just… Sometimes as you grow up, bad things happen."

"Like cancer?"

"Like cancer," Cody agreed, "and car crashes, and bad days at school, and feeling stupid, and—"

Everett tapped his hand. "You can't say 'stupid'. Aunt Kaddy says it's a bad word."

Cody took a deep breath as he processed that. "Okay, fine, some days you feel bad, or lonely, or unwanted. That's part of life. Usually it balances out, like a see-saw. Have you seen one of those?"

Everett nodded. "They have one in the baby's wing. It's pink and has spotted dinosaurs on it. But you can't ride it if you're over twenty kilos."

"Pretend the seesaw is life," Cody said as he led Everett out of the snow. "It's supposed to go up and down. That makes it fun, right?"

Everett nodded.

"If one side gets weighed down too much, you get bored. The seesaw stops moving. If it's all good things happening, you might get bored and go looking for trouble. But, if it's all bad things, sometimes you just give up on the seesaw. You decide it's better to forget you can play fun games, because you think it'll be easier. It will hurt less if you pretend having fun isn't an option."

"Does it help?" Everett asked.

Cody took a deep breath. "Honestly? No. You just freeze up, like the glaciers. Water is a bit like us, you know? Water can be light as air, or drip-like, or carve rocks with a stream. It can make unique snowflakes, or it can freeze, tighten, crush itself under the weight of life and become a glacier."

"Glaciers carve rocks too," Everett said.

"And there are times when being a glacier is good," Cody agreed. "But even a glacier becomes a babbling stream again, singing a silly song and playing with the fish."

They walked up to the atrium where Kaddy was waiting by a little wishing pond under the shade of a fake tree. She smiled and waved.

Everett waved back. He hurried through the doors, snow trailing behind him. He hugged Kaddy and she told him something. Everett nodded and hurried back to Cody. "Thank you for coming a second time, Polar Terror."

"Not a problem," Cody said. "I like visiting you." He tried to get a read on Kaddy's expression, but it wasn't working. She'd put her polite smile back on and there was nothing to work with. "Can I walk you upstairs? I need to talk to Aunt Kaddy before I go, if that's all right?"

Everett nodded quickly.

Kaddy shrugged.

Stomach twisting into a knot, Cody followed them up the escalator to their floor. The quiet gave them an illusion of privacy.

As soon as they reached the room, Kaddy sent Everett off to the bathroom to change, and closed the curtain between the tiny living space and Everett's de facto bedroom. "What did you want to talk about?"

"I—" He held up a hand. "Wait." He stripped off the mask and baclava. There was a moment of fear when he wondered how Kaddy would react, but like she had before, she met his eyes without hesitation. He risked a cautious smile. "Does this even the playing field?"

A small smile curved her kissable lips. "It does. Thank you."

"I was going to tell Everett I could come back next week—we haven't had a chance to do the candy shop heist he wanted—but I wasn't sure if that's what you wanted. Do you want me… to stay away?"

"Oh!" She pivoted away, shook her head, and turned back. "I'm sorry, I just… I don't want us to be a bother. It wasn't safe for you to come here today and—" She shook her head again. "You're obviously a very generous person. I don't want to impose. It's easy to take, and there's no way we can repay you for your time."

Cody shrugged, feeling a little helpless. No one had ever acted concerned about how he spent his time before, except for maybe the intervention officer at his high school. But that had been years ago. "Winter's my down season. I have a few things I'll do, photography classes and what not, but most of the winter I just sit at home."

"Oh." Kaddy nibbled on her lower lip as she thought about that. "Still… There has to be something better to do than sit around a hospital all day."

"Sure," he agreed. "Taking Everett sledding, flirting with you, making ice sculptures, maybe catching a hockey game? We could do that indoors, no mask."

She raised a skeptical eyebrow. "What about hiding your eye color from everyone?"

"I'll wear some sunglasses."

"All right." She nodded, the small smile teasing him. "When do we get to see you again?"

Cody thought about his plans. It wasn't a full plan yet, more like a vague sketch of thirty percent of a plan, but the goal was fully envisioned. He was going to grant Everett's wish and make sure Kaddy had an amazing birthday. And if he could win more than a smile from her, so much the better.

Doing that would take some work.

"Tuesday, maybe? Wednesday at the latest. I have to run down to Vancouver."

"For what?"

To have a chat with someone who knew why Everett had gotten a tainted bone sample, but Kaddy didn't need to know that. Cody widened his eyes and put on an innocent smile. "To get candy. For a candy store. So Everett can rob it."

Kaddy crossed her arms and put on a Mom Look. "I can see your eyes. I can tell when you're lying."

"If I promise it's nothing bad, would you believe me?" His grin widened.

"If it's a date, just say so. We don't have any claim on your time."

"You think I'm flirting with you and keeping someone in Vancouver?" He couldn't help but sound amused. "I've been accused of some pretty heinous things, but never that."

She huffed. "The Polar Terror, I'd trust. You're"—her hand made a wobbly circle in the air—"Cody the Cosplayer. Who apparently has a lot of free time and money."

Cody smirked in amusement. He'd made armed assassins tremble and run in terror when they looked him in the eye and Kaddy was talking to him like he was a wayward college student who needed to be reminded to be serious and stop spending their money on chips.

"Am I wrong?" Kaddy asked.

He lifted a shoulder. "A little. But I can understand why you think that. I'll bring references next time, and candy."

Everett peeked around the corner of the curtain. "Are you coming back?"

"Next week," Cody promised. He held up his hand for a high-five. "We'll watch some hockey and read more comics while we make plans. How's that sound?"

"Awesome!" Everett gave him an enthusiastic high five.

Cody nodded to Kaddy. "Have a good night."

"You too. Drive safe." There was a tiny hitch of panic in her voice, but she hid it well.

Cody smiled. "Don't worry. I promise the roads will be perfect tonight." He winked and walked out before she could ask any more questions.

CHAPTER SIX

WINTER LIGHT SNUCK PAST the curtains like a tired kitten. Kaddy lay on the plastic cushion of the hospital bench and watched the light climb the wall as Everett snored. That was something she hadn't thought of in years: light.

Back in high school, she'd taken a photography class and loved it. The interplay of light and shadow, the intricate weave and texture of flower petals and rain drops. She'd loved zooming in on beetles nestled between the stamens of a flower. At fourteen, she'd declared that she'd be a photographer when she grew up. There'd even been a brief search for an art university.

That idea had died within hours.

Her father hadn't approved. Maybe, if he'd lived, she would have felt comfortable fighting him on it. But once her parents died, it seemed cruel to defy them. Although she hadn't stuck strictly with accounting like her mother had wanted. The ecology degree with a math/accounting minor meant she still had some time to play with cameras, it just wasn't as fun.

Sitting up, she stretched and yawned. Maybe she'd buy a camera next year as a present for her and Everett. A gift for their little family if they survived this.

And if she found a new job.

Grimacing, she turned her phone on and opened the email app. Still nothing from the office.

Technically, they couldn't fire her. Technically. But the new budget that had gone through meant that they were downsizing her office, and they didn't need to renew her contract. Three people out of their six-person crew were going to be job hunting by summer. She'd pointed out that at least two of her co-workers wanted to move to bigger cities, and she didn't. But she doubted it would help.

The Yukon was home.

Even Whitehorse felt too crowded most days.

Kaddy turned off her phone. "What I need is someone to pay me to backpack all summer." She smiled at the ridiculousness of the thought. But, who knew? Maybe Cody needed an extra tour guide for his business.

She tried to kill that fantasy before it went too far. Standing up, she stretched again and meandered to the window. Careful to not wake Everett, she pulled the curtain back a tiny bit to peek outside to the parking garage, the city, and the distant snow-capped mountains. Freshly fallen snow blanketed everything except for the top level of the garage, where someone had carved a giant wave of ice and a set of palm trees with a hammock. The rising sun shattered on the ice, making the whole scene glow.

Well, maybe it wouldn't hurt to indulge in a little fantasy.

To: FireFlow@WhiteKnight.net.ca
From: 134235@WhiteKnigth.net.ca

I hear you're the person to talk to if I want info on underground medical equipment, supplies, or other things. I need info for a case. Let's meet.

- The Yukon Kid

To: 134235@WhiteKnigth.net.ca
From: FireFlow@WhiteKnight.net.ca

Vancouver Aquarium
Local Waters
1pm

CODY TUGGED A VANCOUVER Stealth hat low over his eyes as he ducked inside the aquarium's side door. Average Canadian lacrosse fan, that was him.

A gaggle of school kids wearing bright green shirts with penguins on them walked past making sea lion noises. Or screaming. It was hard to tell.

The aquarium wasn't a bad place to meet. Lots of people. Lots of noise. Minimal security, and what security did exist was focused on the tanks and displays, not the people. The security guards were looking for child predators and lost toddlers, not clandestine meetings between superpowered humans.

Although Fireflow probably wasn't going to be fooled.

The Yukon Kid was a teenager with a strong Quebecker accent, the ability to fly, and a cheerful smile.

Cody didn't pay attention to the music industry, but he was pretty sure the Kid was singing with an international boy band these days. Either way, the Yukon Kid didn't look like he was pushing thirty with a five o'clock shadow and a look that chilled the heart.

But Cody was running on the thought that begging forgiveness was better than asking permission.

The exhibit with local marine life was easy enough to find, although "Treasures of the B.C. Coast" sounded like a strip joint more than anything. Educational either way, probably. He followed a group of school children in and looked around, not entirely certain what he was looking for.

Fireflow was a superhero who, according to rumors, could turn fire into water and back again. Handy for fighting wildfires, which is what he assumed she did with her skills. If she'd *set* wildfires, she'd be listed as a super villain.

Not that there was a list that he knew of. Or even a formal way of tracking each other. All the superpowered humans he knew had just sort of found each other. One industrious soul had put together an old-school chat forum, and they had gathered.

No one in the crowd stood out. A spandex uniform would have been nice, but outside the movies, no one really wore those. Something about looking like an escapee from an 80's workout video.

Still, process of elimination… It had to be someone old enough to pay for their own internet, carry their own phone—and Fireflow identified as female. Which narrowed it down to over twenty adult women in the room.

Cody grimaced. *Should have asked her to wear a rose or something.* He ducked his head as a security guard ambled past, and looked around again.

In the far corner, standing by the octopus tank, was a middle-aged woman with blonde hair pulled back in a practical ponytail, bright green eyes, an infectious smile, and a Fireflow fan pin on her purse: the teardrop shape with the distinctive blue bottom and flame-red peak meant the woman was either the superhero or a big fan.

Feigning interest in the exhibit, he slowly made his way to his target.

As he approached, the woman looked up. "The Vancouver Stealth? Really?"

"Not subtle enough?" Cody flashed her a smile.

"You don't look like the Yukon Kid."

"It's a school day. I told him I'd come pick up his mail."

"Yeah." She crossed her arms. "What's with the sunglasses?"

He lifted a shoulder and dropped it in a shrug. "I don't like bright lights."

She looked up at the artificial gloom of the aquarium. "Want a second chance?"

Cody titled his sunglasses down so the superhero could see his eyes.

Fireflow's pupils dilated in fear as her back stiffened. She took in a deep breath.

He pushed his glasses back into place.

"So."

"So," he agreed.

Fireflow shook herself. "I wondered how much of the stories about you were true."

"Most of them," Cody said. "Although I'm a bit more law-abiding than I was in my wild teens."

"And you need… medical help?"

"I need to track an organ donation."

The expression on her face shifted from Scared to Mom Glare in a blink. "For what?"

Cody lifted the corner of his mouth in a sardonic smile. "Believe it or not, to help a kid."

"Put the kid on the waitlist."

"He was on it," Cody said. "But the bone graft he was supposed to get was swapped in transit. Had to have been. I already checked the hospital and chatted with the nurse in charge. The right bone was extracted and packaged for him. But he wound up with a diseased bone and is currently going through chemo. I'd like to have a word with the people who intercepted the shipment."

Fireflow pursed her lips and looked away. "It won't help the boy."

"I know."

"So why do it?"

"Because they might hurt someone else. And because I'm a bad guy. I'm allowed to punch people when I'm angry."

She sighed and started walking slowly.

Cody kept pace.

"I can't advocate violence. Even if you found one of them, there are others. There's a whole ecosystem." Fireflow stopped to watch a tank full of sea urchins.

"Crime is never an isolated event. If only a single person is held accountable, there are enablers all around. Someone in the hospital. Someone harvesting the replacement organs. Someone disrupting the supply line. Someone buying the good organs. Punch one and the others will replace him. They have to. It's a matter of self-preservation."

She pivoted to face him. "Find another way to help the boy."

"No."

Fireflow tilted her head, looking dangerous when she should have looked winsome. "No? What good is violence going to do?"

"Violence? All I need is the threat of violence. Fear, cold as the Arctic winds. That's enough to bring their whole world to its knees."

She raised an eyebrow. "Hmmm."

Cody smiled coldly.

"West End, corner of West Hastings and Cardero, there's a building where a back alley doctor works. It's not far from St Paul's Hospital, and close to the docks and airport. If I were looking for black market organ sales, I'd start there."

"Thank you. That's all I need."

The superhero crossed her arms again. "I'm not going to regret giving you that information, am I?"

"You? No." But someone else would. He'd make sure of that.

CHAPTER SEVEN

KADDY CLOSED THE DOOR to an empty hospital room behind her and unmuted her phone. "How many times have I told you, I can't move to Alberta?"

"It wouldn't need to be long term," John said. Her boss sighed over the phone. "Look, I'm trying to keep you at the same paygrade. They're closing the office up here."

"Why? We're one of three environmental offices in the Yukon. We need *more* field offices, not fewer. Not everything can be done out of Whitehorse!"

"There's a field office up at Fort Good Hope in the Northwest Territories that's going to cover the northern Yukon."

That was still too far away. "What about loaning me out to one of the First Nations? Doesn't someone need an environmental scientist in their area? I could do wildfire recovery or land reclamation. Something. Anything!" There was rent to pay on the house she never slept in because Everett panicked whenever she left him alone. He needed new clothes. She needed new shoes. "John, help me out. What's in the area?"

"Do you have to stay in the Yukon?"

"Everett's doctor is here. Even if he's free to leave the hospital—and we don't know if he will be for weeks—we'll need to come in for regular check-ups. I trust the doctors here. We're close to home and family."

"You're family's dead," John said bluntly.

She held the phone away from her face long enough to growl at it. "So? I like the Yukon! I like being up here. Winter is..." Her gaze drifted to the window and the park where she'd played with Everett and Cody. "Winter is cozy." Especially when there was the option of cuddling with a man with strong arms and a wicked smile.

"There's winter everywhere in Canada."

"You know what I mean."

"No, I don't. Which is why I'm eyeing a job in Barbados. They need environmental scientists too."

"Your specialty is Arctic studies."

John laughed. "Terns migrate, right? Arctic terns? I think I read that somewhere as an undergrad."

Kaddy rolled her eyes. "Is there any way we can keep the station open?"

"Not with the current budget."

"What about Kluane?" Kaddy asked desperately. "One of the park wardens there said they were hiring more staff for the summer season."

"I think that's just rumors," John said, "but I can put out some feelers, if you want. Make a recommendation."

"Please?"

He sighed again. "Fine. I'll see what I can do. I think Mark Haines is in charge of hiring out there. But I'm sending you this list anyway. It covers all of western Canada. You can ignore the options in Alberta and try your luck with the rest. Listen, Kaddy, it's a job. Just... just find one, okay? I feel like a heel calling people the week before Christmas and telling them they only get one more paycheck. I fought for this, for the station. I've called everyone I could think of, and the budget committee chair twice a day. There's no movement. No funding. My wife is already looking for a realtor to sell the house."

Kaddy closed her eyes and sagged against the wall. "I know you did your best. I'll... I'll be fine. Thank you. I better go." She hung up and let gravity drag her down.

The hospital bill wouldn't be a problem. (Thank goodness they weren't from the USA or she'd wind up like that math teacher who made meth. Or chemistry teacher. Or maybe he was a piano teacher? Whatever, she'd seen an episode once while traveling and been shocked by the barbarity of it all.) But there were still other expenses. Severance pay wouldn't last forever, and things had been tight even before this year.

Everett would need some Christmas presents too. They weren't religious, really, but no one liked seeing all the other kids get presents while their stocking remained unstuffed.

Putting her game face back on, Kaddy stood up. The bad news could wait for another day. Right now Everett needed a cheerleader.

The doctors had been talking about another surgery today and Everett was wilting. She'd go be the perky, optimistic aunt with plans to take him camping this summer.

Now, there was an idea: they could head out into the back country and never look back. Subsistence hunting and fishing, forage for some berries, smoke the salmon over a fire. She'd never had to do it for survival, but her dad had taken her hunting during the summers. And practically everyone knew how to fish. During a salmon run, all it took was a net for the fish and some bear spray to stay alive. Easy as pie... which she'd never been able to make without burning.

A strained smile stretched across her face as she walked back into Everett's room. Kaddy opened the door, and to her surprise heard Everett talking animatedly to someone.

"And then, when I get a horse, I'm going to ride it down the Long Canyon Trail. There's gold there, you know? Like from Butch Sundance and the Cassidy Kid!"

"Butch Cassidy and the Sundance Kid?"

Kaddy's heart fluttered with delight. That was Cody's voice. She pulled the curtain back to see Everett and the Polar Terror wearing paper cowboy hats and flipping through a new comic. "Hello."

Cody stood up and tipped his paper hat over the wooden mask he always wore. "Howdy, Miss Kaddy."

"Howdy?" She had to bite her cheek to keep from laughing. "What's this nonsense?"

"A new comic came out so I thought I'd make a surprise delivery," Cody said, grinning from ear to ear.

"The Polar Terror goes back in time to the gold rush to rescue Klondike Kate and stop the nefarious Soapy Smith!" Everett held the book up for her. "This is the best!"

Kaddy nodded in agreement. "Soapy Smith?" She turned her attention to Cody. "Are you scared of baths, Mister Terror?"

The expression on his face went from cheerful to scandalous far too quickly. He coughed, and shook his head as he pushed whatever thought he'd been chasing away. "Soapy Smith was a con man from the States who would wrap money around soap, cover the soap, and then sell the packets off. People paid extra thinking they might get the lucky soap."

"Ah... sounds awful." Kaddy shrugged. "Why's the Polar Terror fighting a swindler?"

"Soapy Smith has a gang," Everett said, not looking up from his brightly-colored reading. "They time traveled to the future, found out about oil, and wanted to chop down all the trees in the north."

"That sounds convoluted, but sure." Comic books made about as much sense as anything did these days.

Cody leaned in close. "Are you okay?"

"Hmm?" She blinked in surprise.

He nodded to the door and gently pushed her away from where Everett was devouring the latest fight, complete word balloons filled with bright red POW!s and BANG!s.

Figuring that Everett wouldn't need her until he ran out of pages, she took the hint and stepped into the hall.

"What's wrong?" Cody asked. "You look upset."

She shrugged. "It's been a long day." She crossed her arms. "Everett might need another surgery. My boss called to tell me I'll need to go job hunting. I still haven't done any Christmas shopping. Just another day in hell. You know how it goes."

"A little bit." He took off his hat and mask. "Anything I can do to make it better?"

"Hmmm... I don't know. How are you at getting government budgets passed?"

"Not great." He smiled and the world seemed a better place. "But there's a hockey game on in an hour and I could pick up some pizza and wings. Or Chinese?"

"Mister Terror, are you trying to bribe me into a good mood?" Kaddy couldn't help but smiling.

He frowned playfully. "I thought you were going to call me Cody from now on."

She lifted a shoulder and dropped it. "I was helping you stay in character."

"Don't worry about me. I can handle myself."

"I'm sure you can." *But I'd like to handle you too.* Much more than was appropriate for a hospital guest helping out a family. Right now it would be so nice to sink into Cody's arms and have someone lie to her, tell her it was all going to work out. Every time she looked into his eyes, she felt overwhelmed by how much she wanted to keep him beside her, like a lucky penny or a stuffed teddy bear.

Cody raised an eyebrow. "You look hungry?"

"Really?" She didn't feel hungry. Not for dinner, at any rate.

He leaned close. "How about I go get food and, if that's not enough, you can take a bite out of me later." He winked.

Kaddy shot him a look that would have made a normal person run.

Cody's grin just widened.

"You think highly of yourself, don't you?"

"Not really, but you don't often find women who want to face off with a super villain."

"Because you're so dangerous?" She couldn't help it, she was closing the space between them.

"Everyone else thinks I am."

Kaddy bumped his nose with hers. "If you're scary, I'm the Blue Fairy."

"I do not get that reference." Cody laughed. "But I'll agree with anything you say."

Reluctantly, she pulled away. "It's a book my sister used to read to Everett. There were magical creatures of every color, and the Blue Fairy is the one who scrambles all of them up, so there's a red lizard and a green polar bear. It's silliness."

"Oh, and we can't have that of course. You're never silly or impulsive."

"Not really."

"I bet I could fix that." He said it so softly she almost wasn't sure what he'd said. But the look in his eyes made it very clear.

There was an invitation there, if she wanted to take him up on it.

"Aunt Kaddy!"

Retreat being the easiest course of action, Kaddy hurried back to Everett's side. "Hey, kiddo. How's the book?"

"Empty." He held up the comic book. "What were you two talking about?"

Cody came back in with a pair of sunglasses on. "We were talking about dinner and a hockey game. What sounds good to you?"

"Wings!" Everett said. "And french fries! And a milkshake. And bread sticks. And candy. And ice cream. And—"

Kaddy held up her hand. "Got it. You're hungry. I'll put an order in at the pizza place down the street."

"Last time it took three hours for the delivery guy to get here," Everett complained. "Can't we just go out?"

"Not tonight."

"How about I go pick up the order while you two set up for the game?" Cody asked.

Kaddy nodded. "Let me get my purse." She pulled out a stack of baby blue five dollars bills. "I have some cash."

"So do I."

She looked up and stared at him in confusion.

Cody looked back her, expression unreadable.

"I don't expect you to pay for our dinner."

He opened his mouth to say something, but shut it as he became aware of Everett gesturing wildly in her peripheral vision.

Kaddy scowled at her nephew. "What are you plotting, young man?"

"Me?" He radiated innocence. "Nothing."

She turned to the Terror. "And you?"

"Nothing planned at all." He was lying, badly. "I'm a modern man. If you want to buy me dinner, I'm not going to say no. But, for the record, I don't kiss on the first date." Cody plucked the cash from her hand with a smile.

Liar, she mouthed.

He lowered his sunglasses and winked.

Kaddy blushed and turned away. Was it wrong to want to flirt? To want to smile? Cody's attention made her happy. But that was wrong, wasn't it?

She shook her head as he left and sank down into her usual chair, resting her eyes for just a moment. The silence passed as it always did in the hospital, full of ticks and beeps and bips.

After a few minutes, Kaddy sighed, and opened her eyes to find Everett studying her. "What?"

"Is it working?"

"Is what working?"

"My wish!"

"What wish?"

Everett tilted his head and sighed. "I wanted you to be happy. For your birthday," he added in a tiny whisper.

Kaddy shook her head. "Ev, sweetie, it's not my birthday! Why are you worried about that right now?"

"Your birthday is soon," he argued. "And you look happy. Why can't we be happy?"

She shifted, standing so she could reposition herself on the edge of his bed. "Aren't we happy?" She said, smoothing back his hair. "I mean, another surgery won't be fun, but the prognosis is good. You're going to get better. You might be able to leave by April. We could move anywhere! Go hiking. Go camping."

Everett kicked at the blankets.

"What else do you want?" Her heart broke. Why wasn't her sister here? Why had she made that dumb phone call that night? If she'd just kept her mouth shut, Everett would never have been hurt. Her sister and brother-in-law would be alive. They could be a real family. "Ev, sweetie, just tell me what it is."

He sighed, frail shoulders slumped forward. "I want to go camping as a family."

"Okay. We'll do that."

"We can't!" His eyes were filling with tears. "I'm not big enough to take care of you if you get hurt. We need another big person. And you… You don't watch enough TV!"

Kaddy blinked in surprise. "TV?"

"On TV, when someone is doing something wrong, there's a commercial or TV show or something that comes on and tells them what to do."

Clearly she hadn't been paying enough attention to his viewing habits. "I guess I didn't know that. What problem am I supposed to get fixed by watching TV?"

"You're supposed to get a boyfriend," Everett said. "Then I approve, and help him pick out a ring, and you get married. And then we have another big person to go camping with us."

"Um… Okay… You know, we can probably get someone to go camping with us without the whole marriage thing. I have friends."

Everett gave her a look of disbelief. "Aunt Kaddy, I have friends. You have mutuals." He patted her hand. "My friend Krissy told me the difference. A friend is a person you see in person and who comes to visit when you're sick. A mutual is someone you talk to online, or see at work or something. No one ever comes to see you, so you don't have friends."

"I have… Andrea?" Kaddy scrambled. "Um, some of the nurses and I are friends?"

He shook his head. "They don't count."

"Work friends?"

"No."

"Cody?"

Everett frowned.

"You know," she said. "The Polar Terror? Can he be my friend and yours?"

Everett's eyes went wide with shock. Very slowly, he turned in the bed to look at her. "He has a name?"

Kaddy nodded.

"He told you his name?"

She nodded again.

The wheels in the seven-year-old's head started turning. "Do you think the Polar Terror likes camping?"

She shrugged. "He seems like a person who would."

"Maybe he'd go camping with us?"

"Maybe. He might even do it without getting married to me."

"But…" Everett smiled slyly, "if you did get married, we get to keep him, right?"

Kaddy pinched his cheek. "I don't think we can keep a super villain. That's not in the rental agreement on the house. No dogs. No cats. No yellow curtains. No super villains."

The door opened and Cody walked in with the food. "No what now?"

Everett leaned forward. "Aunt Kaddy says we can't take you home because the rental agreement doesn't allow super villains."

"The cost of insurance for a super villain's lair is too high," Kaddy said, holding her hands up in apology. "There's just no way to make it work."

"No dogs, cats, yellow curtains, or super villains." Everett sighed. "What about superheroes?"

"Yeah, what about superheroes?" Cody asked. "Are you going to let the Yukon Kid move in with you?"

"Because I need another kid while I'm a single mom?" Kaddy laughed. "Thanks, but I'll pass." She grabbed the edge of the table. "Here, let's set up by the bed so we can watch the game."

Everett grabbed his food and set it up on his tray. "Can we turn the lights off?"

"Sure," Kaddy said, standing.

Cody beat her to the wall. He smirked as he reached for the lights. "You sure you trust me with the lights out?"

"There's a kid in the room," Kaddy said primly.

The Polar Terror looked over at the kid dipping his french fries in ranch dressing. "Wanna bet he falls asleep by the second half?"

"What are we betting?" Kaddy asked.

"A kiss good night."

For a moment she forgot how to breath. A kiss from a villain?

His lips looked soft and inviting. His touch was gentle. He could break her heart, but she knew it was going to end, knew he was going to leave. So what would it hurt? It was a moment of fun, nothing serious.

She didn't have to put her heart on the line.

Kaddy smiled. "You're on."

CHAPTER EIGHT

ON THE SMALL TELEVISION screen, the hockey players hugged and a fight broke out.

Cody stretched, looking back over his shoulder to check on Everett.

The little boy was sprawled on the hospital bed, snoring.

Bumping Kaddy's shoulder, Cody grinned. "Second half. Guess who's asleep?"

Kaddy looked over. "Huh. He must be feeling worse than I thought. He slept most the day." Worry stole her smile away.

"Maybe the hockey game was just that boring," he teased. "You were nodding off too."

"I'm a bad Canadian. I don't love all hockey. Sorry."

"I'm not offended." Cody smiled. "I am curious though."

A small smile tugged at Kaddy's oh-so-kissable lips. "About what?"

"About what it's like to kiss a superhero."

Her eyes went wide as she laughed in surprise. "A superhero? Well, I don't know, I've never met one."

"Mmm, you mean you aren't one." Cody reached for her hand on the floor next to his. "You can tell if someone is good or evil by looking them in the eye, you're working to save the planet, and you adopted your sister's son. You think that's something just anyone would do?"

"Well, I mean, probably? Wouldn't they?"

"Newsflash: not everyone is as selfless and giving as you."

Kaddy shook her head. "No, I think most people would be in my situation. Everett is easy to love."

"So are you." The words slipped out, and he watched as they hit her.

First, there was a look of confusion. Then, she shook her head. Finally, Kaddy looked up at him. "Isn't it a bit early for that? You barely know me."

"Isn't love like that? You find something you want to love, and you want to learn more. You want a kiss because you won a bet."

"I won?" Kaddy teased.

"*I* won." Her lips were tempting him. All he had to do was close the distance between them. "And I want my kiss."

She rolled her eyes, leaned over, and pecked him on the cheek. "Good enough?"

Cody ran his tongue over his teeth. "What do you think?"

Kaddy was nose-to-nose with him, eyes shining. "I think you want more."

"You're right." A terrible thought occurred to him. "Do *you* want more?" If she said no...

The answer was a light kiss on the lips, soft and warm and teasing.

Cody caught her waist and lifted her onto his lap. Tilting his head, he stole another kiss, tongue running along the seam of her mouth.

She opened, letting him in as her arms wrapped around his neck.

"Aunt Kaddy?" Everett said sleepily.

Kaddy pulled away, hurriedly standing up and wiping her mouth. "Right here, baby. What do you need?"

Sleep. Cody stared at the boy, willing him to fall back asleep.

Everett yawned and sat up. "I'm hungry again."

"We've got plenty leftover. Want me to heat something up?" Kaddy asked.

"Do we have apples?" Everett asked.

"There are some down in the common room," Kaddy said. "Do you want an apple while we watch the game?"

Everett grimaced at the TV. "Could we play a game?"

"Sure thing," Kaddy said.

"Twenty questions is always fun," Cody said, unprompted. "Or truth or dare."

Kaddy hid a smile behind a cough.

Mmmhmmm. She could pretend all she wanted. There'd been a spark in that kiss, and she'd been just as invested as he was. All that was left was convincing Kaddy to do the one thing no one else in the world would do: love him enough to stay with him.

THE NEXT MORNING KADDY woke with a smile. It was the sunshine, she told herself. Waking up to a bright morning and the smell of fresh flowers in the hall.

She licked her lips, and the memory of kisses stole her breath again. A teasing kiss during the hockey game. A stolen kiss as they answered Everett's questions about favorite colors and favorite movies. A hundred imagined kisses every time she met Cody's eyes.

The pure pleasure of human touch meant to do more than push her aside so a nurse could rush in.

It was selfish. It was greedy. It was wonderful.

Kaddy sighed and leaned back in the seat by the hospital bed as the nurses whisked Everett away to be weighed again. For a few minutes last night, she'd been more than Everett's legal guardian, or a worried family member, or even an aunt. She'd been Kaddy, just Kaddy, for the length of a kiss.

"This is ridiculous," she muttered to herself.

Of course she was flustered. Everyone liked attention. Love was one of those basic human needs, like air and water.

And, if things were different, maybe she'd let things play out. Go on a few dates. Pretend that she and Ev were going to have a normal life after everything they'd been through. But dragging someone else into this mess? No job. No promise of recovery. No house soon enough.

No one deserved to be saddled with her debts and problems.

Especially not someone like Cody, who was giving up so much of his time to be here and entertain Everett.

Grumbling as her dreams burned to ash, she reached for her laptop. If she could get a job then at least that worry would be gone.

Everett came back, walking slowly. He closed the door with a sigh.

"What's wrong, kiddo?"

"I'm bored." He sat down beside her. "When's the Polar Terror coming back?"

Kaddy shook her head. "I don't know. He said maybe later this week. But he has work too. He doesn't get paid to come here and hang out with us."

Everett frowned.

"He'll be back," she promised. "He still has to run a candy store heist with you."

That didn't seem to be the right answer. Everett curled in on himself.

"What's wrong?"

"Can we make him stay?" Everett asked. "Like, forever?"

"I…" Kaddy shook her head. "Like, have him work here at the hospital? All the time? I don't think he'd like that job. He's a photographer."

Everett's face turned red with anger. "Not work here. Stay with us. When we leave. I'm getting better. I am, Aunt Kaddy, I can feel it. I'm going to be all better soon."

She bit her lips, hoping and praying he was right.

"Couldn't the Polar Terror be my daddy? Then he could tell me stories every night."

"You have a daddy, Ev."

"I want a live daddy! I want one I can remember."

Her heart broke all over again. "Oh, Ev. Do you want to look at pictures?"

"NO!" He stood up. Outside, as if to match his mood, a heavy wind bent the trees. "I want another family. Not just my dead mom and dad, but live ones too! It happens! I've seen it happen! People on TV get new parents all the time!"

She closed her eyes and wished a thousand painful deaths on every producer of cheesy kids' shows where new parents magically appeared. "It's not that easy, honey. I love you to pieces. I'm… I'm sorry. Getting you a new daddy is a lot harder than just asking for one."

Everett stomped over to the window to watch the wind blow the snow around. "You don't care. You won't even be my mom."

"That's not fair!" Kaddy put her laptop to the side. "You're my sister's baby. I don't want you to forget her. She loved you so much, Everett. You were all her hopes and dreams come true."

"But you don't love me."

"I do!"

He turned with tears in his eyes. "Then why can't I be your baby too? Why can't we be a real family? Why do you have to be just my aunt?"

She went over and hugged him. "I'll be more than just your aunt, okay? If that's what you want, I'll be your mom too. I just…" *Don't want to think your mom hates me. It's bad enough I lived when she died. How unfair is it to steal her son's love?*

Hugging Everett tighter, she stared out into the settling snow.

Would a sign be too much to ask for? A little hint that her sister was okay with her being more than the distant aunt?

She kissed Everett's head.

He looked up at her, pouting. "So, you'll be my mom?"

"Yes, I'll be your mom."

"Good." He smiled. "That means the Polar Terror can be my dad."

CHAPTER NINE

"WHAT?!"

Everett crossed his arms. "I saw him kiss you. That means he *loves* you. That means you'll get married. I could get a brother!" His widened in excitement. "Or a sister." He frowned. "I guess a sister would be okay."

Kaddy laughed. "Slow down, kiddo. A kiss doesn't mean true love or marriage. He was flirting. Playing. Being silly."

"What?" Everett sounded disgusted. "That's not right. Kisses are for people you love. They aren't for playtime."

"Yeah, well, it's a little more complicated when you're an adult. Lots of things are more complicated when you're an adult."

"Why?"

She shook her head as she sat down beside him. "Who knows. One of the mysteries of the universe, I guess."

Everett crossed his arms as he considered this. "But… He kissed you!"

"Mm hmmm."

"So, is that like, a maybe he likes you?"

"I guess," Kaddy agreed.

"So, *maybe* he'd want to be our family's daddy?"

A memory of sitting in Cody's lap, his arms wrapped around her tight, and a hungry kiss stole her breath away. For a moment she'd been the center of someone's world. The undivided focus of someone's attention… Just thinking about it made her want to run into Cody's arms again.

"Maybe," she said. "It's not something we want to rush into."

Everett sighed dramatically. "Do you think he'll come visit again soon?"

"I don't know." And, like an idiot, she hadn't thought to ask for his phone number or email. Andrea, the dream coordinator, probably had it on file. But going down and asking for it would mean dealing with Andrea and Andrea's questions. She patted Everett's good leg.

"When's your birthday?" Everett asked out of nowhere.

She frowned at him. "Earlier this year."

The weight of seven-year-old's glare was heavier than the threat of a super villain playing in the hospital. "Aunt Kaddy, I know it's this week."

"Do you?"

"It's Thursday. It was on the charts the nurses have."

She rolled her eyes skyward. "Yeah. I guess it's this week. But it's not a big deal."

"The Polar Terror will be back for that," Everett said with a calm surety.

"It's okay if he isn't."

Everett grinned in a way he probably thought was sneaky. "Yeah. Fine. We're not doing anything at all."

It sounded like there was a surprise party in the planning. She'd have a quiet word with the nurses, and

Cody if she saw him, and put a stop to it. Surprise parties never ended well.

Her mom had planned one for her thirteenth birthday, and that had ended with her father having a heart attack.

On her sixteenth birthday, the surprise had been her mother's funeral.

And then her sister had tried to surprise her for a lonely birthday in college and a drunk driver had ruined that too.

Birthdays never brought good surprises.

VISITING HOURS RAN FROM ten to three. The nurses made the rounds at eight, noon, four, and a final evening check at eight. Which is why any sound the door made at nine forty-five was ominous.

In Kaddy's experience, it meant that something had gone wrong with the morning check-up. An hour from nurse's station to in-house lab, and then a consult, and then down to Dr. Kobbler's office for the nine fifteen reports, and then...

Dr. Kobbler peeked his head in. "Hello. How is everyone?" He was smiling, an improvement over his usual somber visage on days like this.

"Everett's taking a little nap," Kaddy said. "He's hoping he'll have visitors today." Or *a* visitor at any rate.

"Could you step outside for a moment?" Dr. Kobbler asked.

Letting go of her laptop was like throwing her security blanket in the trash, but Kaddy did it. She set it down, walked outside, and stepped into the tiny conference room that smelled of lemon floor polish and tears. It was the room where all the families went when the doctor had news it was best the child didn't hear.

Dr. Kobbler pulled a chair out for her.

Kaddy stayed standing.

He smiled in understanding. "This is not bad news, per se."

"Is it good news?" Kaddy asked.

The doctor sighed. "It's news. The bad news is, after consulting with some of my colleagues and looking at Everett's latest set of x-rays, I don't think he's fit for another surgery or bone transplant."

She bit the inside of her lip to keep from crying.

"He's seven, and still growing, and there are concerns about how he's been growing. Even after we took out the, uh, let's say rancid bone, his body is reacting differently than we expected."

"How differently?"

"Not bad," Dr. Kobbler said quickly. "But it seems to be healing better than we thought it would. Filling in more than we'd expect to see. It's not unheard of, but when you have the bell curve of recovery, we don't plan on the patients being over-achievers. But, Everett is."

Visions of math and statistics swam in her head, but it didn't really make sense. "What's it mean?"

"It means we'll probably be fitting Everett for a brace in about three weeks. There's a fellow in Haines Junction who has a 3D printer, got it to make braces for his elderly dog, there was a fundraiser online and donations and—" The doctor saw her blank expression and smiled sheepishly. "It's a cute story. Well, the upshot is, he had an excess of donations and contacted all the local hospitals to tell us he can make custom casts and braces."

Dr. Kobbler pulled a piece of paper from his pocket, unfolded it, and handed it to Kaddy. "It's an open honeycomb design. Snaps right over the leg, light-weight, but protects the weak bone like an exoskeleton. It can get muddy, wet, whatever. Everett will be able to wear it under his clothes."

Kaddy looked at the design. "Okay... I guess." She frowned. "When will it get muddy?"

"Ah." The doctor smiled. "That's the other news, and this bit is good. Everett's test results came back negative."

The word fell into a blank space in her mind. "Negative?"

"His white blood cell counts are normal. There's no decay in the bone. Tuesday will be Everett's last round of chemo. We'll keep him here for a little bit longer, and then he'll be able to go home."

"Home?" The enormity of it sunk in. They could go home. Home to... nowhere. The rent was overdue. There was no paycheck coming in after the first.

The hospital was home.

Kaddy sat down.

"He'll need regular follow-up visits and tests. Every two weeks to start, then once a month, then we'll stretch it out to six months," Dr. Kobbler continued, oblivious to her distress. "I recommend continuing the online schooling until the end of summer, and he isn't a good candidate for the live virus vaccines for another year.

But he should be able to attend a normal school in the fall."

"I..." Kaddy blinked. "I..."

The doctor patted her hand. "It's been a long road. Give yourself some time to think about it."

One thought managed to gain dominance. "No more surgeries? Ever?"

"I'm recommending we don't schedule any more for at least a few years. It depends on how he's growing. The leg will be weak. There could be problems later on. But, with physical therapy and standard precautions, he should be able to have a normal childhood. I'd discourage you from enrolling him in anything where he'd get kicked a lot. Swimming would be a good sport."

"Hiking?"

"He should be able to hike by this summer," Dr. Kobbler said. "He'll need to work up to it. He's been in the hospital for nearly a year, remember that. He won't have the energy or strength overnight. But, short hikes? Day trips? Easy things like that? Absolutely doable."

"And... long term?"

The doctor shrugged. "Barring any sudden changes, he'll have a full and happy life as long as he makes healthy choices."

She wiped away happy tears. "Oh... I just... I was preparing for the worst, you know? All this time I tried to believe it would be okay, but I was braced for bad news. I don't know... I don't know what to think."

"Try not to," the doctor advised. "I'll give the good news to Everett later this week once everything is formally signed off by his team. We'll plan a celebration for him then. In the meantime, I'll have the nursing staff prep the release forms, and schedule follow-ups.

"He'll be moving from chemotherapy down to the second floor rehab rooms in two weeks. We'll do strength training and endurance to start. Work on rebuilding his energy and introducing a wider range of foods to his diet."

"Wonderful." Three weeks to find a job and housing.

There was a polite knock at the door and Andrea poked her head in. "Good morning!"

If Kaddy could just siphon off some of that bubbly cheer, she'd have a wonder drug with a street value that would keep her in money for life.

"Is this a bad time?" Andrea asked.

"Not at all!" Dr. Kobbler said. "I was giving Miss Chaak an update about Everett's prognosis. We have some good news to celebrate later. What brings you up here?"

Andrea slipped into the room. "We have a bit of news from Vancouver. One of the couriers that handles transport of live tissue went to the police today and reported that he'd been paid five thousand to redirect a shipment of certified healthy bone. He was given an unverified replacement."

"Everett's transplant?" Kaddy guessed.

Andrea nodded. "It seems likely, although the police and hospital admin are still fact-checking."

"Good grief," Dr. Kobbler said. "What would possess someone to do that? There's plenty of bone grafts to go around."

"Who knows?" Andrea shrugged. "But the courier's guess is that the bone graft originally intended to come here went south across the border."

Kaddy crossed her arms and tried not to think about it. "Why did he come forward?" It wasn't like anyone had looked into it. Oh, Dr. Kobbler had made phone calls and someone down in Vancouver had lost their job, but everyone had put it down to casual incompetence. Theft and bribery, that was a whole other matter—one no one had seriously considered.

All the courier had to do was keep his mouth shut and spend the money.

"The detective I spoke with said the courier was shaking and terrified. Someone put the fear of God into him."

"Nice to know that religion still works for people," Kaddy muttered. "Bit late for Everett though." But maybe it would save someone else. Keep another family safe and happy.

Dr. Kobbler smiled. "Well, maybe we have the Polar Terror to thank." He chuckled. "That's one of his talents, isn't it? Scaring people with his eyes or something?"

Kaddy forced a smile at the joke. "Sure. He came here and was so charmed by Everett he decided to go fight bad guys in British Columbia for us."

"Um." Andrea's smile looked painfully forced. "Ha. Ha. Funny. Ha."

Kaddy laughed. "What? You don't like having a super villain here?"

"Not really," the dream coordinator said.

"Oh, he's just a man in a costume," Dr. Kobbler said. "Superpowers aren't real."

Andrea's smile reached a brittle breaking point. "Uh huh. Of course. He only looks scary."

That did make Kaddy laugh. It was impossible tp picture Cody scaring anyone, let alone a real criminal.

"I should get going," Kaddy said. "Get some emails read before Everett wakes up for lunch."

Dr. Kobbler nodded. "Good. Good. I'll come by tomorrow with some paperwork and the new treatment plan. Look for me around, oh, eleven-ish probably. Andrea, would you be so good as to accompany me downstairs? I need to talk with the Montagu family this morning. More good news! They say these things come in threes, don't they?"

Threes? Andrea watched the pair walk off. Why couldn't one of the three be a job interview up here in the Yukon? Would it really ruin some divine design if she had everything all at once?

Sighing, she walked back to the hospital room and sat down in the gloom.

Maybe there was something to the theory that there was only a finite amount of happiness in the world. Maybe she'd already used all hers up having Everett healthy again.

"Come on, world, give me just a little bit more. Give me a way to make a home for Everett."

She opened her laptop and scrolled back up through her emails.

At the very top, the newest one read: JOB INTERVIEW – PRINCE GEORGE

CHAPTER TEN

ANDREA WATCHED AS KADDY frantically stuffed half her wardrobe into a duffle bag at the edge of Everett's bed, dump it out, and try again.

The kid watched with a worried expression.

Finally, Andrea sighed. "Are you sure about this?"

"Yes! The weather is good. I have a flight—"

"You have a jump seat on the mail plane," Andrea said. "That doesn't count as a flight."

Kaddy held up two nearly-identical gray shirts. "The Mackelsons are flying back tonight. Mail plane down. Back with the Macks. All I have to do is dazzle them in this interview and it's all done. Easy-peasy."

"Then why are you packing?" Everett asked.

"Can't they do it by Skype like normal people?" Andrea asked. The whole idea of flying in this weather gave her the heebie-jeebies. The Pelly Mountains weren't meant for flying over anyway. They were meant for climbing. "We almost have Everett's candy store set up. Doctor Kobbler is excited. The Polar Terror is coming…" She let that bit dangle so she could get a reaction.

Not that it was any of her business who the patient's families made friends with, but the Polar Terror had been showing up a lot more than he was scheduled to. He made Kaddy smile and Everett laugh, which was the only reason she hadn't kicked the masked man's balls through his nose. He still hadn't filled out all the required volunteer forms.

Kaddy hesitated for a fraction of a second and shook her head. "I've got to get this job. And they said they can't Skype. The president is some quirky white guy who thinks he belongs in Seattle and eschews technology. That's the word they used, eschews." She blinked. "Americans are weird."

Andrea looked into the hall where a nurse was pushing a cart full of meds. There was probably something unethical about tranqing Kaddy at this point, although it was a tempting idea.

"Listen, Ev, I'll be back by midnight," Kaddy said. "Miss Andrea is going to keep you company and introduce you to the new physical therapist. We'll change rooms on Saturday. Good? Good."

Everett gave her a doubtful look. "Good luck," he finally said.

Kaddy leaned over and kissed his head. "I'll be back in no time."

"Have a good flight," Andrea said lamely. "Good luck with the interview."

As Kaddy vanished down the hall, Everett held up a pair of high-heeled boots. "She took her joggers."

Andrea shrugged. "Anyone who *eschews* technology doesn't deserve to see a woman in cute shoes. He probably eats crickets and talks about the natural forces of cavemen." She sat on the bed with a sigh. "Well, whataya want to do, kiddo? Ready for a round of Uno?"

Everett leaned forward, mimicking his aunt's most interrogating look. "Rumor has it that someone donated a VR set to the hospital, and a new video game."

"You only talk to me for my tech." Andrea laughed. "Let me get you a wheelchair. I'll take you down to the new high-tech toy room."

HOAR FROST CLUNG TO the mostly naked street trees, lining them with white crystals that sparkled in the falling light. Out of habit, Kaddy checked her phone to see the time. Almost four in the afternoon and they still had daylight, lucky dogs. Sunset at home was already in full swing behind the heavy gray clouds she'd barely escaped.

Traveling twenty-five hundred kilometers south would do that.

She switched her duffle to her left hand and searched through her phone for directions to her meeting. Underfoot, the snow swallowed every sound. If she didn't look up, she could forget anyone else in the world existed.

The taxi had dropped her off at the car rental place on Queensway, but the meeting was at city hall five blocks away. According to her phone, it was an easy walk, even in winter. Feeling slightly smug that she'd saved herself some money for a nice dinner, Kaddy walked down the street, watching the holiday lights wink on as the sun fell in the west.

This wasn't the pretty end of town. The buildings were all the boxy, easy-to-build style seen in every town that grew too fast. There was a PowerPro warehouse, a wheel place offering a deal on late-season snow tires and chains, and a beige-and-green building with a dome that broke up the monotony and offered a parking lot with a few cars instead of the ubiquitous trucks.

Kaddy's phone chimed.

Incoming Message: Location Change – Meet At Ramada – President's Suite – Top Floor

A twist of worry knotted in her stomach. Meetings in hotel rooms were never good. But, the boss was flying into town. And even if it was a government-funded job, it didn't mean they had stable offices at City Hall. Things could have happened. Maybe a pipe had burst. Or someone had put a computer in the tech-free room the boss wanted.

She texted back. "Understood. On my way."

Turning north on 4th Street, she walked along the side of a hotel that looked like a multi-layer brick-and-window sandwich, dirty snow crunching under her shoes.

The hotel clerk behind the long counter welcomed her with a disdainful sneer.

"I'm meeting someone upstairs," Kaddy said.

The clerk rolled her eyes and muttered something that almost sounded like, "Who orders ugly hookers?"

But that wasn't possible. It was her own unease playing games with her mind.

Kaddy stepped into the elevator and checked herself in the mirrors. Okay, her ponytail looked a little frizzy. But hat hair was one of the acceptable abominations of winter.

Her coat, though, was a faded green, a little too large and old to be stylish. Kaddy unzipped it and stuffed it in the duffle bag, with her wallet and her spare clothes. The dark green blouse she'd picked out was professional, even elegant. Her jeans were dark and clean, her boots perfect for the weather.

"So maybe I'm not a California model, but they aren't hiring a model, they're hiring an ecologist." Her fingers found the chain for the golden eagle necklace her college advisor had given her as a good luck charm.

The elevator stopped and the doors opened to reveal four large men in dark suits waiting for her.

Kaddy's fingers tightened around the handles of her bag. It wasn't much, but they probably weren't expecting anyone to hit back.

"Miss Chaak." The man pronounced it like Jack, which was just as well.

The original census worker who had written down her distant ancestor's name hadn't known the language. And no one in the family had ever felt a need to go fix the record.

"Mister Hoffman is waiting for you."

"I wasn't expecting such an entourage," Kaddy said, lifting her chin. "Do you all work for him?"

The speaker nodded. He was a bland-faced man who would blend into the background of any bar in North America. Hair shaved short, skin tanned but not dark enough that he couldn't pass as white, muscular build. In a leather shirt, he could be a dancer; in a suit, he looked like security. But the way he moved said he'd been trained in some form of martial arts.

"Are you traveling alone?" Something in his tone raised the hairs on the back of her neck.

Kaddy forced a smile. "No. My friends came with. Who wouldn't want a weekend in the city? They're checking into our hotel room. Once this interview is over, we're going to dinner."

"Which hotel?" the man asked.

"Does it matter? Is there a place I shouldn't be staying?"

"Mister Hoffman can pay for your hotel," the man said.

Kaddy chuckled. "That's a generous offer, and—if I take the job—I'll let the company cover my future business expenses. But this is just an interview. Let's not get ahead of ourselves." She patted his bulky arm and made eye contact.

The man's eyes were an empty, watery gray. In Cody's eyes she saw a bright future, sunshine, hope, love. In this man's eyes she saw snow and ice, silence and screams, fear and fury.

She laughed again to hide the shiver sliding down her spine. "Do you do Cross Fit? You've got nice biceps."

"Mister Hoffman requires his security detail to stay fit."

"If I get this job, do I get a security detail?" The trick with predators was to keep them confident. Let him think he had the upper hand, that she didn't know something was wrong. She was watching the rest of the men, checking for exits. It probably wasn't more than someone who thought they could pressure her into a little sex for a job, but ecologists made enemies.

Last summer she'd gotten death threats after turning in a report that limited the expansion of a mining operation north of Grand Forks. The year before that, her whole office was audited after a logging baron complained to a friend in the government that they'd maliciously prevented him acquiring more land.

Hoffman had responded to her resume quickly. Maybe too quickly.

The security man smiled as he steered her towards the suite door. "If the interview goes well, I'm sure I'll see you more."

Kaddy shot him a flirty smile. "I'd like that." *Especially if I were behind the wheel of a truck and only saw you in the rearview mirror.*

The security man knocked and a voice inside said, "Come in."

"Mister Hoffman will see you now."

Kaddy slipped her thumb across her phone and turned on the recording. Time to see who wanted to play games with a Yukon girl.

CHAPTER ELEVEN

THERE WAS A HALO around the winter sun that gave the courtyard of the hospital a fey glow. Cody took the stairs two at a time, not slowing at the check-in desk. By now everyone knew who the Polar Terror was going to visit. Even the bags he was carrying didn't bother them.

He had everything for Everett's candy shop, and for Kaddy's birthday. A present for her might mean a kiss for him. That hope had kept him buoyant all week, even if a sense of dread had hunted his every breath.

All humans had more than five senses—everyone knew that—but he seemed to have a sense most people didn't. One of his foster moms said it was religious, God trying to warn him, but who knew. He didn't seem like the type any god would want to talk to.

Still, it was there, a sense of what was about to happen. Like a spider could anticipate the movement of prey, Cody knew when trouble was coming. And it was coming now.

As he waited for the elevator, he looked around, trying to pinpoint the source of his anxiety.

Everything was quiet at work.

The problems with Everett's bone donor had been solved. Fireflow's information had been good, and the person he'd sent to the police had enough information to bring the whole organization down.

And yet…

He rubbed a hand across the back of his neck. Maybe it was just the season. Birthdays. Winter holidays. The new year. It was a time for family and hope, and he was in the hospital feeling like the last puppy at the pet store.

The hall to Everett's room seemed unusually quiet. It was never loud at the best of times, but usually the quiet was cut by the murmur of conversation or the soft clicking of Kaddy's laptop keyboard. Today, there was nothing.

Cody knocked on the hospital room door, rocking on his heels. How was this supposed to go? Was he supposed to ask Kaddy if she wanted to have a serious relationship, or should he ask Everett if it was okay first? How did people figure out they were dating? Or was he too old for dating?

Movies made this look so much easier than it was. Because, "Hi, I think I'm in love with you, can we keep seeing each other?" didn't sound like it was going to work.

As the door opened his throat tightened. What if Kaddy said no? "Um, hi, K—" He stopped and stared at the short woman waiting in the room. "Is Kaddy here?"

"No," Andrea said as she opened the door the rest of the way, "she had to go to Prince George for something. I told her I'd sit with Everett."

Cody walked into the room and saw Everett on the bed pouting. "What's wrong, kiddo?"

"Aunt Kaddy ran off in a hurry. She didn't even take her good shoes!"

"She said it was a work interview," Andrea said with a shrug. "They were supposed to Skype but something came up. She wound up hopping on the mail plane."

Cody frowned. "The mail plane? Is that legal?"

"For short hops and small towns they'll take passengers if there's room or there's an emergency. The planes are the only way in or out of town until spring." The Dream Coordinator gave him a telling look. "I'm amazed you're able to travel."

"I don't always use a car," Cody said. It was truthful enough.

Everett looked over and sighed dramatically. "She ran off! Aunt Kaddy knew we had a planning meeting today and she ran off!"

"I'm sure it was important," Cody said. "Do you know which company she was going to talk to?"

Everett shook his head.

"Hoffman and Barrow," Andrea said. "I saw the email before she closed it. They have offices in Vancouver, she said, but that's all I know."

"Hoffman?" He'd heard that name recently. But where?

Andrea clapped her hands. "Oh! Before I forget! I need you to sign a consent form."

"Forms?" Cody put the weight of his distaste into the words.

"In this case, the hospital wants permission to use your likeness on the hospital website." She pulled out her phone and thumbed through, then turned the screen to show him a picture of Kaddy, Everett, and himself playing outside in the snow. "We like to show people what volunteers can do. It's not just medical professionals who help these kids heal. Donors, volunteers, and supportive communities all contribute to recovery."

Hoffman. The informant he'd tracked down and sent to the police said the man he reported to worked on the corner of Hoffman and Barrow.

"Do you like it?" Andrea asked.

He stared down at the picture. "Is that up already?"

"Yes. Why?" She scowled at him. "You're the one who always dodges my requests for paperwork. And you have a mask on! Why does it matter? Is this going to break your modeling contract?"

"How long has it been up?" Cody pressed.

"Um... a day or two?"

"And Kaddy left this morning? Without warning?"

Andrea nodded, obviously hearing something in his tone that worried her.

"I've got to go," Cody said.

"But you just got here!"

He was already running down the hall. Prince George was only two thousand kilometers away. *Only.* "You idiot," he told himself. "What were you doing, thinking you could have happily ever after?"

"I'M AN ENVIRONMENTAL SCIENTIST, not a vet," Kaddy said as the doors shut behind her. "Did you need to bring the bulldogs?"

The man sitting in the hotel suite was the picture of All-American, with blond hair swept to the side, blue eyes, a navy suit and pinstripe tie. He had the tan of someone who went yachting for fun. His smile would have fit James Bond or a villain-of-the-day from any of half a dozen TV shows.

She stopped well out of his reach, but far enough from the door that she'd hear it open before anyone could reach her. "Why'd you bring the bodyguards to a job interview?"

All-American smirked. "You're in the same field as me. Haven't you had a few death threats? A coal miner angry you're shutting down his line of work? An oil baron angry you won't let him expand into virgin territory? Death threats happen."

Kaddy nodded curtly and folded her arms. "I've had a few, usually by email."

"With recognition comes more direct forms of threats." The man spread his hands as if that explained it all. "You should know that. You spend time with dangerous criminals."

Worry forced her to frown. "Criminals?" Kaddy racked her brain. "Do you mean Doctor Arthur? That was her research, and she had every right to disseminate it as she saw fit. Just because your government wanted to use the study as leverage for political concessions doesn't mean a Canadian scientist has to listen. I know she's not allowed to travel through the USA anymore, but she's hardly a criminal."

The man chuckled. It wasn't a comforting sound.

None of this was comforting. The room was dark except for a slit of sunlight coming in between the heavy curtains. The heavy wood paneling and over-sized hardwood chairs of the suite gave the whole place a grave formality.

With extra emphasis on the grave.

Kaddy rolled her shoulders back. "Did you need me to come to Prince George to check my references? I thought someone from HR could handle that from somewhere warmer."

"Doctor Arthur isn't the concern," the man said. "Our company's concern is that, while very qualified, you are the caregiver for a little boy with bone cancer."

"He's recovering," Kaddy said quickly. "And there are rules, you can't make a hiring decision based on my nephew's health."

"But we can make a decision based on the fact you spend time with a dangerous man."

She shook her head, beyond puzzled. "Who?"

"Kodiak Old Crow."

Kaddy blinked in confusion. "Cody... ak? Kodiak Old Crow?" She cleared her throat. "The Polar Terror?"

The man in the chair nodded.

"He's a comic book character. I don't think he even has his own cartoon."

"A man matching his description threatened a courier in Vancouver. The courier turned himself into the police, saying that he'd been paid to divert hospital-grade transplant material."

Her heart sank as the room grew cold.

"The only case that man handled was a bone graft. Can you guess where it was headed?"

"No," Kaddy said. "I don't—I don't pay attention to those things. The doctor in the hospital said we needed a bone graft, and we got one. I don't know anything about where it came from." Her heart raced in fear, but her voice stayed steady. "What could this possibly have to do with me? I've never even been to Vancouver. How would I know the courier?"

"You know the Polar Terror." The man pulled a tablet off the table and turned it on.

An image of the Polar Terror standing near a truck dock and a scared young man filled the screen.

"So?" Bravado kept her going. "A man in a fur coat and a man in a baseball hat. Is it a drug deal? Are they smuggling exotic animals across the border? What has this got to do with me?"

The man's smile was colder than the snow outside. "What would draw the attention of a man like the Polar Terror?"

"Nothing," Kaddy said in the same tone she used to cut off Everett's arguments. "Because he's not a real person. He's fictional. Like Batman and Wonder Woman. You do realize that, don't you? I'm here for a business interview, and you're quizzing me about a fictional super villain who has fought Bigfoot and Snow Sirens. I understand our industry has its fair share of conspiracy theorists, but this is a bit much. If you want to talk about environmental science, fine, talk. If you want to keep nattering about your imaginary friends, you need someone with a degree in psychology, not ecology."

She turned around and headed for the door.

"You know him, Miss Chaak. We have proof."

Kaddy looked over her shoulder to where Hoffman's screen now showed a promotional picture of Kaddy, Everett, and Cody playing in the snow. Someone must have taken it from the observation deck. Cody hadn't mentioned enemies, but then again, anyone who thought the Polar Terror was real probably didn't need an excuse to hate him. "You have a picture of a three people in snow gear in the Yukon. So what?"

"So what?" Hoffman's demeanor cracked a little and anger peeked through. "This man matches the description of the man who intimidated our courier. Terrifying eyes, brown hair, and Yukon furs."

"That describes eighty percent of Canadians," Kaddy said, sidling toward the door. "This isn't Norway." The 'our courier' bit was a concern for later. Perfect cover though. An international businessman bringing back specimens for an ecology study could easily smuggle organs.

Hoffman surged to his feet. "You will tell us everything you know about Kodiak Old Crow!"

Kaddy grabbed the door and opened it fast. "Sure. I've read the comics to my nephew a billion times. I can rattle off everything you need to know."

The blond bulldog stepped into view. "Mister Hoffman—"

She brought her bag up fast, slamming it into his chin, and then sprinted away as the bulldog stumbled back. Someone had once said that foot chases never lasted long—most people couldn't run forever. Her run was about to end at the elevator.

Grabbing the corner, she spun down the far hall and rushed towards the service staircase.

In case of fire...

She smashed the cover over the fire alarm with her purse and pulled the alarm. If this wasn't an emergency, nothing was.

Sirens wailed and water sprinklers dropped, spraying everything.

Kaddy pushed open the staircase door and saw another group of guards. "Help! Mister Hoffman is under attack!" She pointed desperately back the way she'd come. "He told me to run!"

The well-trained idiots rushed past her.

She jumped down two landings, skidding and sliding, and opened the door to the fourth floor as the door above her opened with an angry shout.

Fourth floor. Locked doors all over the place. And a pool.

Not super helpful.

Where was everyone? There wasn't a house cleaner or hotel staffer in sight.

She turned the corner and a hand wrapped around her wrist. Kaddy brought her purse up as she turned to her attacker.

And Cody caught it with a smile. "Hi."

CHAPTER TWELVE

Cody's smile faded as Kaddy stared up at him in wide-eyed panic. "Cody? What are you doing here?"

"Um... I thought maybe you'd need a ride or something?" Even to him the excuse sounded weak. But somehow 'I thought you might get killed because of me' didn't sound any more plausible. He reached for her arm, and she pulled away.

"Are you with Hoffman?"

"Who?"

The door slammed open and a group of men in fitted black suits swarmed out.

Kaddy stumbled backward, then turned, running away from him and the men with guns.

Frustrated, Cody pulled on the water vapor coming from the humid pool room. A sheet of ice crashed through the glass and barred the hall.

"What—" Kaddy spun and stared.

"We should go," Cody said, grabbing her hand.

"What is going on?" Kaddy screamed. "I came for a job interview, and now I'm being chased by someone who thinks you're a... you're a..." She stared at the wall of ice.

Cody raised an eyebrow. "A super villain?"

"That's… There's a logical reason for this. Isn't there?"

He nodded. "Yes. I can control cold weather, make things freeze, terrify people by looking them in the eye, and you're being targeted because I shut down a black market organ theft ring."

Kaddy closed her eyes and squeezed his hand. "How do you say that so calmly? How did you do that?"

A bullet thudded into the wall of ice.

A small crack formed.

"Can we go now?" Cody begged.

"Since when were you a superhero?" Kaddy demanded.

"Since… forever? I was born this way." He looked nervously at the wall. "Look, this is not the time or place for a dramatic coming out scene. You're in danger because of me, and I promise, as soon as you're safe I'll disappear. I'll—"

She moved too fast for him to duck the slap that caught the side of his head and made his ears ring.

Cody widened his eyes. "Um…"

"You are an idiot," Kaddy said with careful enunciation. "Did I blame you for this? Did I tell you to leave? No. I asked for an explanation. I thought you were a cosplayer! Some super-devoted fan who had memorized comic books! Couldn't you have hinted a little bit? Maybe made a rose out of ice or something cliché like that?"

"I didn't think you'd like that." The ice was cracking. "Can we discuss this later? Somewhere safer? Safer is key here," he added, tugging on her hand.

"Can't you quick-heal or something?"

"Yes," Cody said. "Can you?"

It was Kaddy's turn to look discomfited.

"Then let's go and you can chew me out later."

Finally the fact that the ice might break seemed to sink in, and Kaddy nodded. "Right. We should go. Elevator or the other stairs?"

"The stairs are fine." Cody maneuvered himself so he was between her and the angry men. "Faster, please."

Kaddy turned the corner as he heard the ice crack.

Angry shouting filled the air.

"Someone will call the police, won't they?" Kaddy looked up at him with a worried expression. "All this noise…"

"I don't know if anyone else is here."

"But, downstairs—"

"There was no one at the front desk when I came in."

The floor shuddered under their feet.

Cody raised his hand and sent an icy blast of arctic air to take out a hotel room door and the window beyond. A twist of thought and a spiraling slide of ice formed. "Hurry. Go down."

"I..." Kaddy hesitated only a moment before shaking her head in bewilderment and sliding down, duffle bag on her lap.

He followed, and as soon as he was down he let the slide fall into a ramp of snow. "Did you bring a car?"

"I took a shuttle to the rental place, but it was easier to walk." She looked up at the window. "Are they going to jump?"

"Possibly." *Definitely.* Whoever was after him and Kaddy had hired some very loyal, very reckless help.

The first grunt landed with a soft puff of white snow. The others followed.

"Kaddy, I need you to close your eyes."

"What? Why?"

He could feel her body heat behind him, almost close enough to touch. *Almost.* "Do it, please."

"Sure."

Cody pulled off his sunglasses and glared. It didn't sound dramatic, but being born with a gift for the evil stink-eye of doom wasn't something most people would brag about anyway. He felt nothing.

But Hoffman's soldiers? They trembled. They hesitated. They looked away, terror telegraphed in every movement.

"Do not come any closer," Cody ordered.

Thirty men with weapons shuffled backward in knee-deep drifts.

"That's so weird," Kaddy muttered. "They shouldn't be doing that."

"Didn't I—" Cody caught himself before he turned. He couldn't look at her.

But she was already there. Meeting his gaze without hesitation. "Why would I close my eyes?"

"Never mind," Cody said with a sigh. "Let's just back away slowly and get out of here."

The ground shuddered again.

A man stepped into view above them, framed by the broken glass of the hotel room window.

"That's Hoffman," Kaddy said. "He brought me here for an interview, but then all he did was ask questions about you." Her voice creaked, and a quiet laugh escaped into the frozen battlefield. "Oh, gosh, how cliché can this get? I'm the superhero's girlfriend who gets kidnapped by the villain."

A fist hit his shoulder.

"What did I do?" Cody asked.

"If you'd told me you were a real super"—she fumbled at the word hero—"*whatever*, I would have planned ahead! Secret identities get girlfriends killed."

Despite the severity of the situation, Cody grinned. "You're my girlfriend now?"

Kaddy's eyes went wide with surprise and pain. "I just..." She looked away. "Sorry. It was just a kiss or two. I guess I read into it—"

He grabbed her hand and pulled her to his side for a hug. "I love it." He wished his super power was stopping time because all he wanted to do was stop and kiss her breathless.

She blushed as she smiled.

Hoffman chose that moment to leap into the pack of silent goons.

"Perfectly good romantic interlude ruined by idiot," Cody muttered. "The title of my memoir is going to be *My Life As A Comic Book Cliché*."

"Polar Terror," Hoffman said.

The voice was unfamiliar. Cody tilted his head. "Who are you?"

The ground shook and the men who had been trembling stood straighter.

Hoffman smiled. "I am what you only pretended to be. Powerful. Strong. Wealthy."

"I never pretended to be wealthy," Cody said. "And I'm strong enough. Let Kaddy go, and you and I can discuss the rest somewhere else. Prince George doesn't have the budget for street repairs, so we're not doing a showdown here."

"You are going nowhere. Neither of you. This city is mine. These people are mine."

For the first time, Cody noticed a ring of people gathering along the sidewalk. They were wearing office clothes and jeans, parkas and sweaters. Some of them were barefoot.

All of them were watching Cody intently.

Kaddy held onto him tighter. "What is he doing?"

"No idea. Super powers don't exactly come with a training manual, and it's not like you can search people like him up on Wikipedia."

There weren't many options. If help came, it wasn't going to be from the local constabulary.

"Okay," Cody said. "I have an idea that you may not love."

"Does it involve both of us getting out of here alive?" Kaddy asked. "Because that's my primary concern right now. Those people look ready to rip our limbs off."

"Yeah, hold on to me."

She smiled. "I like that idea. What's the part I won't like?"

He raised an eyebrow. "Ever flown on the Arctic wind?"

THERE WERE NOT ENOUGH coats in the world to make flying warm. She could feel the weight of Cody's arm around her. She could feel muscle under her hands where she gripped his arm. But she couldn't see him.

They'd been standing behind the hotel, surrounded by mind-controlled minions, and then everything had gone the same dark blue as Cody's eyes, and very, very cold.

She shivered. The air burned her lungs with a frosty fire. Her fingers lost feeling and her wrists ached. Just as her eyes started to ice closed, the landscape shifted and she was standing on a thin veneer of ice in the middle of an open plain, covered in snow.

"Are you all right?" Cody asked, looking completely unfazed. "Kaddy?" He put his hands over hers and rubbed the warmth back into them. "Come on. I need you to be okay."

Kaddy managed to nod her head slowly. "So. Cold."

"I know. I'm sorry." He wrapped her in a hug.

She burrowed her face into his coat. "Where are we?"

"About a third of the way to the hospital. Still south of the British Columbia-Yukon border. I wasn't sure... I've never tried to travel with anyone before."

"I'm okay." It was mostly true. "Do you think—"

There was the whumping-thump of something heavy landing nearby, like a giant cat or a heavy suitcase. Or an angry villain.

Cody held her tighter. "While I deal with him, you head out. There's a town about two kilometers east of here. The trail's clear. This is their landing strip, and they make sure it's accessible in case of emergencies."

She wanted to protest, but he was already stripping off his coat and wrapping it around her.

"Go! You have to get back to Everett." Cody pushed her towards the treeline.

Carefully flexing her fingers, she turned, brain scrambling to process everything. They were in a valley. Snow-shrouded mountains with heavy clouds overhead. The temperature was below freezing, but not so cold it would kill her quickly. But Cody?

Hoffman was stalking across the snow, glaring. It was probably some contest of wills. At least, it would have been in a comic book. There would have been squiggly yellow lines radiating off the villains, and maybe some red waves meant to show the strength of the invisible attacks.

But this was real life.

"I am not being scared off by some darn American." Tightening her grip on the duffle bag, she walked slowly, trying to circle around Hoffman without drawing his attention.

"Wait." She shook her head. "This is bad idea. This is... Wow. Too many cartoons, lady. What do we do when we're in trouble? We call the Mounties." She took her phone out and dialed.

"Mount Halfast Emergency Line," a helpful voice said. "This is Flo, what can I do for you?"

"I'm at the airfield, I think. Someone attacked my boyfriend and he's"—on his knees holding his head in pain—"sick. Can you send someone?"

"The airfield?" the woman asked. "How'd you get out there?"

Kaddy looked at the pristine snow. "We were... paragliding? Drifted off course? I don't know, exactly, I might have been drugged."

"Okay," the woman said. "I'll send help your way. Do you have warm clothes?"

"Yes." But the temperature was dropping. Cody was fighting back in his own way. "Can you get here quickly?"

"Shouldn't be more than twenty minutes," the woman said. Then the phone died.

Kaddy glared down at the useless hunk of tech in frustration. Twenty minutes? In sub-zero weather? With a mad man?

She dropped her phone in her bag, zipped it tight, and moved forward.

Nothing hits like an angry Yukon girl who is tired of being pushed around. Kaddy didn't slow down as she approached Hoffman. Running was impossible, but she had some speed and her bag swung at his head to connect with a crack.

Dazed, the villain fell backward.

Cody looked up. "That's not running away."

Kaddy held out a hand for him. "I'm not letting you die."

"I wasn't dying, I was distracting him!" He climbed to his feet and rubbed his head. "Son of a birch tree. I have such a headache."

"What was he doing to you?"

"Pulling on memories. I think he was trying to find a time I really wanted to obey, or when I really loved someone. But..." Cody shook his head. "Did you kill him?"

Kaddy felt dizzy at the thought. "I hope not! I only wanted to knock him out. He might have a concussion though. Do you think I'll get in trouble for that?"

Hoffman groaned. "Why?"

"Why?" Kaddy's voice reached a pitch Broadway sopranos could only dream about. "You stole my nephew's bone graft, lied about a job interview, and threatened me! And you're asking why?"

"Why won't you listen?" Hoffman asked. "I'm a good person. I want to help you." He sat up and looked at her. "All I want to do is make things right."

"Kaddy," Cody's voice had a note of warning.

"Make things right?" She pushed Cody back. "Is that what you think this is?"

"Help me up," Hoffman said. "Listen to me. You are a good person. You want to help me. You will be so happy if you listen to me."

Kaddy rolled her eyes. "I should have brought duct tape."

"Why won't you listen to me?" Hoffman demanded as the snow quivered. "Who are you?"

"Me? I'm a single mom of an adopted kid, an orphan, a survivor, a Yukoner. Which makes me heaps better than a piece of trash like you. Shut up."

Hoffman opened his mouth.

"Shut up!" Kaddy ordered.

Cody chuckled.

"You think this is funny?"

He nodded. "A little. This guy had a whole town obeying him, and you don't even notice. Everyone who looks me in the eyes feels unforgettable terror. Except you. Know what that means?"

"I have common sense?"

Cody grinned. "I'm dating a superhero."

"What? No." She shook her head. "I'm just an ordinary person."

"Uh huh." Cody snickered. "You keep saying that."

She rolled her eyes as Cody stepped closer. "How are we going to explain all this?"

Cody took her hand. "Don't worry. I have a friend here." He kissed her cheek and gave her hand a squeeze. "We'll be okay."

CHAPTER THIRTEEN

"EVERETT!" KADDY RUSHED INTO the room. Worry had gnawed at her the whole trip home, but there he was, looking healthier than when she'd left.

"Aunt Kaddy!" Everett held his arms up for a hug. "I got to see my new room today! It's got a TV bike!"

"A TV bike?

Andrea smiled from her seat on the couch. "It's a stationary bike that powers a screen when he pedals. He'll be able to use it for very limited amounts of time to start, but as he gets ready to leave the hospital, he'll be strong enough to use it more often."

"That's great," Kaddy said. She collapsed onto the edge of Everett's bed.

"You're home early," Andrea said. "We haven't even had dinner yet. Did the interview go well?"

"Uh..." Kaddy grimaced. "It didn't go as expected. The guy who was interviewing me gave off a weird vibe. I would have been a bad fit for the company, I think." That certainly made more sense than trying to explain the truth. The last thing she needed was for the hospital staff to decide she was mentally unfit to care for Everett.

Her nephew patted her hand. "It'll be okay. You don't need a job right now, do you?"

With a weak smile, Kaddy shook her head. "It'll be fine. I actually hopped on a park service flight home. Their fire suppression team was headed up here, and one of them gave me a line on a job."

"The fire suppression team?" Andrea wrinkled her nose in confusion. "Why are the wildfire teams flying anywhere in December?"

Kaddy shrugged. "Team training? Who knows. I didn't ask." The woman Cody had only introduced as Flo had volunteered to give her a flight back to the valley, and Kaddy had been too tired to question anything. "Honestly, today was a little weird. I'm glad to be back so I can get some sleep."

Belatedly, she noticed the lumpy mess covered by a spare sheet in the corner. Everett and Andrea were both trying very hard not to look at it.

"What's that?" Kaddy asked, pointing at the mess.

Everett's eyes went wide in innocence. "What's what?"

"It's nothing," Andrea said in the same breath. "Just a little art project for later."

There was a beep and Andrea hurried to check her phone. "Hey! Look at that, the pizza is here. How about we go have dinner with the other families celebrating today?"

"Yes!" Everett said with an eager nod. "We should do that!"

Kaddy narrowed her eyes. "Are you two plotting something?"

"Yes," Andrea said as she stood up. "We're plotting dinner."

Everett crawled out of bed. He looked excited and cheerful, but a little counter in Kaddy's head was running the countdown to when he'd be out of energy. Out of spoons, in the slang of the chronically ill. He'd had a busy day while she'd been gone.

"You sure you have the energy for this, kiddo?"

"I'll be fine," Everett said. "I took a good nap."

"Okay. Do you want your chair?"

He frowned. "Yeah, maybe."

"He did a short physical therapy session," Andrea said. "They had him on the treadmill trying to get a look at his gait and measuring his endurance."

"I'm doing pretty good," Everett reported. "I'm just sore."

"I'll get you another ice pack after dinner," Kaddy said as she helped him into his chair.

Andrea led the way down the hall into the elevator, and out to the reception wing where the hospital's sterile playground was housed.

Bright overhead lights and carefully chosen living trees planted around the edge gave the illusion of an outdoor space without the risk associated with actually being in an uncontrolled environment. The playground equipment was sanitized every two hours by a machine the kids loved to watch from behind the glass, a mobile car wash with bright pink bubbles.

Most of the children were in the loose, summer-green sweat pants and shirts the hospital provided to long-term patients. Several had face masks on. Caregivers were wearing booties over their shoes, and one had gloves on.

It was at the same time one of the most hopeful things and one of the most depressing. Recovery was a long, dangerous road when the immune system wasn't running as well as it should.

Kaddy pushed Everett up to one of the round tables covered with a plastic tablecloth. There were inexpertly-wrapped presents, a stack of purple plates, and rows of white plastic cups. "This looks suspiciously like a party, and not just pizza."

Everett giggled.

A wave of whispers all around them caught her attention, and she turned.

Cody was standing in the doorway in his full Polar Terror regalia. And he was carrying something that looked very suspiciously like a cake box.

"You did not..." The words were a hiss under her breath.

"Happy birthday, Aunt Kaddy!" Everett screamed.

There was a chorus of birthday wishes and then someone started singing that song.

Cursing the Hill sisters and everyone else who had a hand in popularizing the infernal song in western culture, Kaddy forced a smile. She'd been ambushed. Again. Twice in one day.

"Kodiak Old Crow," she said as Cody walked over, "if that is cake I will take back every nice thing I ever said about you."

He grinned as he opened the box, revealing an assortment of confections from cheesecake bites to chocolates to chubby macaroons to caramel apple slices and chocolate-dipped strawberries. "Happy birthday, hero."

She stuck out her tongue at him.

"What?" Everett asked. "Why'd you call her that?"

Cody grinned at him. "It's always the superhero who defeats the villain and turns him into a good person, isn't it?"

Kaddy took a caramel apple slice and rolled her eyes. "You were always a good person. I didn't have anything to do with that."

"You're still my favorite superhero." He leaned over and gave her a chaste peck on the cheek. "Ev, want to help me hand these out?"

"Yes, then I can help Miss Andrea hang up the birthday games. I drew a donkey and a birthday banner and cut out snowflakes!" He grinned up at her. "Happy birthday, Aunt Kaddy."

She ran a hand through his hair. "Thanks, sweetie. I appreciate this." Emotions threatened to choke her. It was hard, so hard, not to cry. Not to notice all the people who weren't here. But... earlier today it hadn't looked like she was going to make it at all, and yet here she was. Alive. Safe. Welcomed. Loved.

Girls like her, fighting to survive in the Yukon, they didn't always get happy endings. No one was handing out happily ever afters. But with a super villain by her side, maybe she could steal one.

LATER, AFTER THE PARTY died down and the tables were cleaned, they went back to Everett's room.

This was the hard part. This was where decisions had to be made. What she felt for Cody meant nothing if Everett couldn't be around him.

Her nephew climbed sleepily onto his bed.

"You did it," Cody said to him. "You pulled off your villanous scheme."

Everett beamed with the angelic grin of a small child who had gotten away with something devilish. "I'm a good villain, aren't I, Aunt Kaddy?"

"Good villains are usually called heroes." She folded the sheet and dropped it in the laundry basket for the cleaning staff. "Now, are you ready for a present?"

"I get a present?" Everett asked. "Why?"

She licked her lips, unsure how to proceed. It had all sounded so simple in her head. "Well..."

"Would you like me to stick around?" Cody asked as he sat down by the bed.

Everett nodded eagerly.

"We want you to see Cody's eyes," Kaddy said. "You'll be one of only two people who knows the color of the Polar Terror's eyes. Because, well, if Cody is around more, he can't wear the costume all the time." And if Cody's gaze terrified Everett the way it did everyone else, everything was over. Her heart was racing in fear. This was so important to her, and she was helpless.

She couldn't control who Cody was.

She couldn't control how Everett felt.

She couldn't do anything but watch as her hopes and dreams balanced on a knife's edge.

Kaddy closed her eyes and silently prayed like she hadn't prayed since the night her sister had died all those years ago.

Please. Please let this be okay. Please don't leave me alone. Please. Please. Please.

"Ready?" Cody asked.

"Yup!" Everett folded his hands on his lap and watched with rapt attention.

Cody glanced over at Kaddy, flashed her a smile, and took off his mask and balaclava. "All right. Here we go. My best Polar Terror glare."

A chill filled the room.

Shivering, Kaddy crossed her arms, anxiously waiting for something to happen.

Everett frowned. "I thought they'd be brown."

Cody glanced at her. "Okay. And... anything else? Are you scared? Do you feel like running away? Do you want to cry?"

"No." Everett's frown deepened. "Why would I?"

"Most people think I'm scary," Cody said. "But I guess it's a genetic thing. Your aunt doesn't think I'm scary either."

Everett laughed. "Aunt Kaddy's not scared of nothing!"

She rolled her eyes. "Everett! What did I say about quoting TV shows?"

"Only do it if they're grammatically correct?"

"Yes!" She made a mental note to have Everett catch up with his online schoolwork when they had some free time.

"What happens now?" he asked.

Kaddy shrugged. "We'll play it by ear. I still have to sort out a job. And Cody has his own life. But—"

"You're dating?" Everett covered his mouth in excitement. "You're dating? I'm getting a daddy?" He was shaking with excitement. "I'm getting a daddy! This is the best day ever!"

Cody chuckled. "Um, I think you're supposed to wait until I give her a ring before you say that."

Everett shook his head. "No, I already figured it out. You're perfect for Aunt Kaddy. You make her smile, and laugh, and be silly. She's never silly," he said in a breathless rush. "We talked about this! She's going to adopt me and be my live mommy, and that means you'll be my daddy. It's decided."

"Is it?" Cody laughed and nodded along before glancing over at Kaddy in confusion.

"You've been kidnapped," she explained.

"I should at least get you flowers or something." Cody held out his hand. There was an arctic breeze as fog formed and crystalized into a perfect, glacier-blue rose.

Everett's eyes went wide. "Wait."

Cody held the flower out to her. "Kaddy Chaak, will you go out with me?"

"So cliché." She plucked the cold stem from his hand and leaned over to kiss his forehead. "Yes, I will go out with you."

"That's real ice!" Everett shrieked. "He really made ice appear!"

"Yup," Kaddy said. "He does that sometimes."

"Oh, wow!" Everett said, bouncing in delight. "You're the real Polar Terror! My dad is going to be a super villain!"

"Hero," Kaddy corrected. "The ones who stay are heroes." She kissed Cody's cheek. A Yukon girl could have everything after all. All she had to do was love the cold.

CHAPTER FOURTEEN
18 MONTHS LATER

BIRDS CHATTERING SOFTLY IN the forest canopy woke Kaddy from a quiet sleep. She kept her eyes closed, savoring the absence of hospital sounds. Cody's heavy arm was draped over her. Their blankets were soft and smelled of campfire and pine. She could hear Everett stirring in the tent next to theirs.

A rustle of comic book pages, a giggle, and a whisper as Everett read the story again to Charlie, his service dog.

Leaving the hospital hadn't been easy. After nearly a year of constant attention and care, the sudden absence made Everett anxious. There was residual psychological fallout. The doctor didn't want to call it PTSD, but car rides, and being away from her, made Everett's heart race.

Charlie, a two-year-old German Shepherd mix was the compromise, a constant companion who could fetch Everett's braces in the early days, who slept in Everett's bed, and who kept him safe from bears, moose, and mountain lions when the family went backpacking over the summer.

All summer.

"And then Winter Wind…" The rest of Everett's sentence faded out of hearing, but she knew the story.

Winter Wind and the Yukon Cub; they'd appeared in the comic book last spring, just as Everett was leaving the hospital. The creators of the Polar Terror comic said he was getting a fresh new look, an updated uniform, and a family.

When asked, Cody had smiled and said nothing.

His arm tightened around her, pulling her back to the heat of his chest. Soft lips kissed her neck. "Good morning, beautiful."

"Good morning." Kaddy snuggled in, safe and happy. She opened her eyes and saw the silhouettes of Everett and Charlie perk up. They'd been spotted. "And we will have company in three… two…"

Everett jumped to his feet and she heard the bracken cracking as he ran to her.

Charlie woofed softly and ran after him, skidding to a halt at the tent door.

"Morning, kiddo," Cody said with a lazy yawn.

"Mom! Dad! Charlie an' I were reading this one. I opened it last night." Everett kicked off his boots and Kaddy pulled the corner of the blanket back so he could curl up by her.

Cody reached across and tousled Everett's overgrown hair.

It needed a trim when they got back to civilization. But that was a worry for another time.

"What's that?" Cody asked, propping himself on an elbow.

Kaddy grinned. She was effectively pinned between her husband and her son. She looked up, and Cody winked down at her.

"The Winter Wind gets trapped in the badlands of British Columbia—"

"There are badlands?" Kaddy asked. "What is this, the wild west? Are we in Texas now?"

"Arizona has badlands," Cody said. "And BC has deserts."

Kaddy rolled her eyes.

"She's trapped," Everett said loudly over them, "and so the Polar Terror and the Yukon Cub have to go to save her, and everyone thinks the Yukon Cub is the Polar Terror's son since they look so alike, and no one knows the Cub is adopted." Everett beamed at the full-color pages. "It kinda looks like me, doesn't it?"

"Very much like you," Kaddy agreed.

"I'm going to go as the Yukon Cub for Halloween," Everett said with a decisive nod.

"Again?"

He kept nodding.

"I guess I can go as the Polar Terror," Cody said with a serious look on his face. "Think I could pull it off?"

"Maybe," Everett said. "But you have to look grumpy. You're not good at grumpy."

Kaddy subsided into a fit of giggles. "You two are ridiculous!"

"That's why you love us." Cody leaned down and kissed her.

Everett sighed and rolled his eyes. "I'm going to go find breakfast."

"We'll be out in a minute," Kaddy promised.

Cody shook his head as Everett tied his shoes.

Kaddy nodded.

"Where's the fun in that?" Cody whispered as he settled in beside her, hand sliding under her shirt.

Pulling his head down, she kissed him, her hero. "Yukon's best Bad Boy. Are you trying to get me in trouble?"

Another lingering kiss. "How could I be trouble? I'm your loving, devoted husband. I hardly ever do anything wrong."

"Charlie! Not the bacon!" Everett yelled.

Cody broke the kiss with a laugh. "I love family camping trips."

"Yes, you do. That's why we've been out here for three weeks."

"I have my camera! It counts as work." He brushed a hair from her face. "Have I told you today that you're beautiful?"

"Only once." She looked deep into his eyes and saw her future there: beautiful, happy, and just a little bit fantastic.

CLAIM YOUR FREE EBOOK!

THANK YOU FOR BUYING this book!

When you buy an Inkprint Press book in print, we like to thank you by offering you the ebook for free. Please head to:

http://www.inkprintpress.com/liana-brooks/the-polar-terror/

and use the coupon POLARPRINT to download your free copy in both .mobi and .epub formats. (The coupon will only work once.)

ABOUT THE AUTHOR

LIANA BROOKS NEVER INTENDED to live near the Arctic Circle. In fact, she was adamant throughout her life that she never wanted to live north of San Francisco. Life doesn't always turn out the way we plan though and in the mid-twentyteens, Liana moved from the frozen wastelands of the great plains to the rugged mountains of Alaska.

It was cold. It was gray. It was muddy. She learned to love it anyway.

The moose are cute, the summers are gorgeous, and there's nothing like a drive through the bush of Alaska or Yukon Territory to make someone appreciate the natural beauty of the far north.

While she was in Alaska, ensconced in very warm study and hiding under a pile of blankets, Liana came across a Tumblr post talking about the Make-A-Wish Foundation and what would happen if a real supervillain showed up. The rest is history.

Liana now lives a little farther south in a quaint, Pacific Northwest town called Seattle with her family, dog, and framed pictures of a moose in her living room.

For all the latest news, subscribe to Liana's newsletter at www.lianabrooks.com

CHAPTER ONE

I knew from the first time I saw my wife that I wanted her naked. Of course, seven minutes later I wanted revenge. It wasn't that she had handed me my first defeat or ruined my chances for world domination that year, it was the way she kissed me goodbye. She sent my head spinning, then walked away as if I were the least important person in the world.

Once my arm healed, I stole some new equipment, cloned some new minions, and I felt a little different.

I wanted revenge, with a side order of naked.

ACROSS THE DINNER table, Tabitha devoured him with dark, ocean-blue eyes. She put a bite of lettuce in her mouth, full lips pursing around it. Eating salad never looked so good. Her tongue darted out to lick away a stray drop of dressing. She winked at him, promising with every move to do the same to him. "It's almost bedtime," she said, her voice husky and luscious.

"I don't wanna go to bed!" one of the quads screamed.

"What about cake? Don't we get birthday cake?" another asked.

Evan winked back at his wife from the far side of the table, separated by a few feet and four precocious just-turned-five-year-olds, all as stunning as their mother with big, round eyes and hair that fell in loose curls meant to trap hairbrushes and sticky substances. He had to peek at the eyes to see who was talking. Maria had green eyes, Angela's eyes were blue like Tabitha's, Delilah's eyes were brown like his, and Blessing—their stillborn who miraculously survived—had purple eyes. The waif in question had blue eyes.

"Angela," Evan said, "after dinner it's pajama time, and then story time."

"Mommy doesn't have a bedtime!" Angela wailed.

Tabitha winked at him again. "Tell you what, tonight Mommy will go to bed the same time you do. Right after we eat cake." She leaned over to give Angela a hug.

All Evan could see was the deep V plunge of her tight blue shirt. Oh, yeah. Crime didn't always pay, but altering someone's moral compass sure put the O's back in the bedroom.

The cake was split into fourths, equal parts purple, white, green, and blue so each girl could have her favorite color in the cake. Baking four cakes was unreasonable; there weren't any grandparents left to celebrate with, and neighbors had an annoying habit of asking uncomfortable questions. Saying little things like, "You look just like Doctor Charm! Do you remember him? Whatever happened to that guy? Do you know how hard it is to put together a good Villains vs. Heroes fantasy league without him?" made for awkward evenings.

So they had a quiet family party. Cake, then presents, after which he hurried the girls off to bed so he could read Dilly Duck's ABCs in record time before rushing to the bedroom, hoping to catch Tabitha still in the shower.

She was already out and wearing a blue satin robe that caressed her skin in exactly the way he wanted to. Rose-scented candles cast sensuous shadows on the walls.

Tabitha turned, lips curved in an inviting smile. Long fingers twined with the sash of her robe. She tossed her honey-blonde hair in the way she always did when she was about to argue, posing with feet apart and one hand casually resting on her waist. "Sweetie, we need to talk."

Evan wiped grease-stained hands on his jeans as he forced a smile. "Sure, babes, anything you want."

"Really?" She slunk forward, all sinewy limbs and doe eyes. "Promise?" Tabitha nuzzled his nose. One hand flirted up the back of his neck to play with his hair. The other traveled downward, right to his zipper.

Oh, yes, the little Morality Machine in the basement was working just fine. Another thirty, maybe forty years of this and he'd consider retiring. Or turning the machine down so his wife wasn't quite a sex kitten every day of the week. Maybe only days with Y in them.

"Sweetie?" She nibbled his ear. "I want to go back to work."

"What?" Evan actually pushed himself away from her, something he wasn't sure was possible in any other circumstance.

Tabitha tucked her chin and pouted.

"Tabby-cat, I love you, but work? I've got my... stuff... in the lab. I'm busy. And we can't afford daycare for the girls. We're barely making ends meet as it is. Do you really want to go back to being Zephyr Girl? Crime fighting is a game for the young, baby. You're not nineteen anymore."

"I'm twenty-nine. A very"—her hips pressed against his tight jeans just so—"very healthy twenty-nine."

He shivered at her touch. "You're cheating."

"I want to do this, Evan." She ground against the thick denim.

"You can do me all you want, baby."

She stepped back, frowning. "I'm serious."

"So am I." Evan sighed, reaching for his wife. "Sweetie, I love you, but what's the point in being a superhero? The government stipend barely covers the dry-cleaning bill. If it's money you want, write another tell-all superhero book. The Spanish Mask sold his third last month."

Tabitha crossed her arms. "I don't want to write another book just for royalties while you're between jobs."

He waved a finger at her. "I'm not between jobs. I work freelance in the computer business. I'm self-employed. That's not the same as being between jobs."

"Between paychecks then."

"We will have a solid income. This project I'm working on, Tabby-cat, it's going to set us up for life. We're never going to worry about money again. I promise. Give me a couple of weeks and everything is going to be perfect." He caught her hand and pulled her into his arms. The faint scent of her spicy perfume left him dizzy with need.

She rested her head on his chest. "I want to save the world. Have you seen the news, Evan? An entire town in Kansas held hostage for a week by a bomb scare before a superhero was able to get in to defuse the situation. A week! I could have that done between grocery shopping and paying the bills. Ten minutes, no pulling punches."

"I know, baby. No one is better at this stuff than you. But I need you at home, Tabby. Having you out there scares me. I'm terrified I'd lose you. Why don't you wait until I finish this project? I'll be done by the time the election rolls around. Two more weeks. Once I get paid we'll look at this again. I have that armor design for you, I just need some time to put it together."

Tabitha sighed. "You've been saying that since we got married."

"Well, my nights are busy." He nibbled her ear as he tugged her sash loose. "Are you complaining?"

Tabitha stretched against him, sending a delightful frisson of lust up his spine. "I thought you gave up the super villain schemes."

He twitched. "I did, baby. Of course I did."

"But you're keeping me here. Isn't that a little selfish? Just a teeny-tiny bit super villain-ish?" She slipped her hand between his pants and his skin.

"Ah!" He caught her hand so he could think clearly. "Not selfish. Necessary. Like oxygen or sex."

"Don't you mean water?"

"No, definitely sex." Evan slid her robe off and tossed it into a corner. "Come here, Tabby-cat, I'll make you purr."

She tugged at his shirt, pulling it up. The shirt joined the robe on the other side of the room. "What are you doing down in that lab?" she asked as her hands drew lazy circles on his back.

Ten seconds, that's all he'd need to get her panties off. Three more to drop his pants. "What was the question?"

"What are you doing in the lab? What's this project?"

"Oh, computer stuff. I told you. To help tally everything on election night. I'm trying to make the process run smoother so we don't have to worry about recounts."

"Hmmm." She gave him a dubious frown.

Tabitha was built like a supermodel and had a superhero name straight from Campy Comics, but her brain was Mensa all the way. "And this computer program has nothing to do with world domination, or get-rich-quick schemes?"

Evan contrived to look wounded. "Tabby-cat, how can you ask that?"

"Because you spent ten years as a villainous criminal mastermind?"

"I wasn't a mastermind, I was a super villain, there's a difference. Masterminds are just thugs with money. My crimes had artistic flare. I was practically Robin Hood! Robbing from the rich and scandalous, and giving to me."

"Robin Hood gave to the poor," Tabitha said with a laugh. "You were never poor."

He caught her hand, pulling her close. "Poor is relative. Besides, I'm reformed now. You showed me the error of my wicked ways. Although"—he leaned in for a kiss—"if you'd like to remind me why I gave up a lucrative life of crime, I have the evening free."

Keep reading!
Head to www.inkprintpress.com/liana-brooks today!